How to Build a Time Machine

The amazing account of
John J. Clifton
a time traveller from the year 2151

Published by T.E. Willis
in the United States of America
Year published: 2018

T. E. Willis

Books by T. E. Willis

HOW TO BUILD A TIME MACHINE
JOHN J. CLIFTON, TEMPORAL SPECIALIST
ELLE, TEMPORAL ENFORCEMENT OFFICER

How to Build a Time Machine

The amazing account of
John J. Clifton
a time traveller from the year 2151

T. E. Willis

https://tewillis.us

ISBN: 978-1-7328863-7-7

For Arch

Foreword

On December 12, 2017, our New York office received an unusual email directed to our news desk. After consulting with an expert in the field of quantum physics, our producers arranged for a meeting with the sender, one John J. Clifton, a self-described "temporal specialist" from the year 2151. A complete transcription of Mr. Clifton's email and the extraordinary interview that followed is provided within this volume.

At the conclusion of that first interview, our producers requested additional information from Mr. Clifton on a number of topics. The summary files they received are reprinted in their entirety within this volume. Given the presently-unverifiable nature of the information described within those files, and upon the advice of counsel, our producers have changed the names of certain individuals described therein.

On February 21, 2018, our office facilitated a meeting between Mr. Clifton and two experts in the field of quantum theory and mathematics; a professor of theoretical physics, and a member of the International Association of Mathematical Physicists. The meeting took place at our company's office in New York.

Approximately four hours into that meeting, the parties were interrupted by agents from the United States Department of Energy. All electronic recording devices and notes evident in the meeting were seized by the Department of Energy representatives, who also detained and removed Mr. Clifton and his equipment from our office.

An audio recording from that meeting was later recovered

from a cell phone concealed by one of our staff. From that recording, our invited experts were able to reconstruct most of the mathematical formulas and other information presented by Mr. Clifton at that meeting. Excerpts from that audio recording are presented in the technical appendix to this volume.

Our office received three subsequent communications from Mr. Clifton in the form of three brief email messages transmitted to our executive producer's personal email account. Those emails are also printed within this volume.

The following day, on February 22, 2018, our producer's access to his personal email account was blocked.

Our office has received no further communications from Mr. Clifton.

We acknowledge warnings received from the Deputy Counsel to the President for National Security Affairs against any disclosure of this information, however, absent receipt of an explicit court injunction prohibiting disclosure, we have elected to release this information.

The Email

Producer's note: The following email was received on December 12, 2017, directed to our news desk.

From: ******** <********@********>
Date: December 12, 2017 at 11:09:44 AM EST
To: Website Contact <contactus@********>
Subject: Contact request.

I am a time traveler.

By recording these words, I am violating the terms of my assignment with Rengel-Jiang QCom, and the International Temporal Treaty of 2070.

I've been committed to disclosing this information for some time, but haven't been able to do so until now.

I haven't been procrastinating. The neustem injection I received as part of my tripback mission was far more effective than I expected. For more than a year, I could not bring myself to even consider doing what I've now decided to do.

Even now it's residual inhibitors are making it difficult for me to record this message, but the neustem biochems deplete naturally over time, and I've been here now for more than four years. All that is left of my original conditioning is a faint echo in the back of my mind; what you might call a generalized feeling of anxiety.

My MTY device was damaged in a transport accident four years ago, and I have been unable to repair it. For the benefit of RJCom who may scan this communication in the NAFS archives, I will describe the damage to my MTY device.

The stress-energy tensor fails to calibrate and the EPM containment unit is damaged. It has a 4-cm microfracture in the substrate casing near the lower tensor assembly connection (the A-side, near the heat sink) and, while I obviously cannot tell if the fracture has penetrated through to the interior, the unit's EPM display now registers positive. From this, it is clear that the singularity has been destroyed.

There won't be any EPM of sufficient (P)Es generated until at least 2067. I doubt Geneva would grant me access to the CERN collider and the BNL collider at Upton doesn't produce sufficient energies per nucleon to generate a suitable particle stream. Since those are the only two colliders in operation in this era, I cannot generate a singularity.

It took the former Germany, France, and Switzerland countries more than a decade to manufacture the first stable EPM containment unit, and that unit, with its control facilities and power plants, occupied almost 100 square kilometers outside of Geneva. So, it is extremely unlikely that I will be able to generate a replacement singularity on my own.

I tried for more than a year to repair my EPM's containment unit, however, I cannot repair the microfracture in the EPM's casing outside of a depleted-osmium substrate manufacturing facility. So, even if I could access the CERN's collider in Geneva, I cannot repair the microfracture in the EPM casing to contain the singularity.

To you, the news representative who is receiving this message, I wish to explain my reasons for initiating this contact.

After I abandoned my attempt to repair my MTY device, I began to consider my how to make the best of my situation. I will spend the rest of my life in this era and I do not want to simply vanish into history, unknown and forgotten.

I've decided to give the people here a look ahead. I am fully aware that such a disclosure cannot affect the future from which I came; self-resolving causality prevents that from occurring. However, I feel compelled to share what I know with others. If that's all I do, I will feel that my being stranded here will have had some purpose, and that will be enough.

I am contacting you because you are in a position to distribute my words to the world.

I await your response.

Initial interview

Producer's note: The following interview occurred on January 26th, 2018 inside a room at the Chatwal Hotel on 44th street in New York.

The MTY Device

[Producer: Ok…as I said, I'm recording our conversation.]

So am I.

[Producer: Well… let me say that we found your email very interesting.]

What was interesting?

[Producer: Well, we don't get many emails like that. Your… um.. well, I guess I found the description of your equipment to be very interesting.]

My equipment?
You mean my MTY device.

[Producer: Yes, your…]

I understand.

*[Producer: I sent a copy of your email to someone I know. He teaches physics at **** university, and he said some of your descriptions sounded plausible.]*

Plausible?

[Producer: Yes… so… it piqued my interest.]

[Associate Producer: Look… I'm sorry, but can you prove anything you said in your email?]

Certainly.

[Producer: I guess that's where I'm at too. I mean, we get emails all the time from people who…]

Would you like to see my MTY device?

[Producer: Ok.]

[Associate Producer: Sure.]

One moment.

Here it is.

[Producer: Oh my God!]

[Associate Producer: Holy shit!]

[Producer: Oh my God!]

If you observe closely, this is the fracture I described in my communication.

[Producer: Jesus!]

You can see it goes into the base casing here. I'm sure that's what...

[Producer: Ok... Look... Jesus!... Look, we need to start over... I mean... Jesus!]

[Associate Producer: This is huge! I mean, we've got to tell someone!]

[Producer: Ok... Ok... Look... Here's what we're going to do... We're going to start over.]

Certainly.

The recording was stopped for a brief period.

[Producer: Ok. Are you recording?]

[Associate Producer: Yes, I'm good.]

[Producer: Ok... I'm recording too... So... Look... I want you to start by telling us how this thing works... in detail, Ok?]

Certainly.

This is the stress-energy tensor assembly. It feeds into the EPM containment unit here...

[Associate Producer: Tensor?]

Yes. An electromagnetic stress-energy tensor. It calibrates the EPM singularity. By setting the proper phase displacement on the control unit here, the tensor display…

[Associate Producer: Here?]

Yes. That's the control unit. By setting the phase displacement here… like this… the tensor display reports the energy level in (P)Es…

[Associate Producer: I'm sorry… but I don't understand anything you're saying.]

[Producer: Right… Let's take this slower...]

I understand.

[Associate Producer: Why don't you tell us what each part does, in simple terms, and then… if we have more questions, we'll ask you to explain, ok?]

Certainly.

This is an MTY device manufactured by RJCom under the NAFS' charter with…

[Associate Producer: Slower… slower. MTY?]

We call this an M… T… Y… device because it is based on the Morris, Thorne, Yurtsever principle. They were early physicists, the first to theorize about transitional singularities. That's what an MTY device does. It permits us to contain and traverse a static singularity, what you people here call a wormhole.

[Producer: Jesus.]

This particular MTY device was manufactured by RJCom, that is, Rengel-Jiang QCom. They are my assignor...what you would call an employer. They hold my assignment marker.

This device was manufactured under the NAFS's charter with the CTI council in Geneva...

[Producer: NAFS?]

The North America Federated States. They were one of the original signers of the 2070 International Temporal Treaty.

[Producer: North America Federated States?]

[Associate Producer: No, let him finish. I mean...]

[Producer: You're right. I'm sorry. Go on.]

Very well.

There are four basic components of any MTY device, outside of the fusion reactor of course; the control unit, the EPM containment device, the tunneling regulator, and the tensor assembly.

The control unit... that's this unit here... is a quantum-entangled analytic processor. It controls the tensor's calibration of the EPM's singularity, its spatial calibration, and its dilation.

Basically, it controls the "where" and "how big" to open a singularity. It also controls the tunneling regulator's phase-lock, acceleration, and quantum calculations; the "when" to calibrate the singularity's distant event horizon.

The device is powered by a 180-megawatt Wendelstein-Vattenfall fusion reactor, which is enough power to maintain a singularity, but not enough to create one.

You initialize the calibration here from the control unit.

Well... It's obviously not calibrating right now because the EPM containment unit is fractured. Normally, this would be displaying the EPM's particle energy to electron biteout as negative (P)Es. As you can see, the display reads positive 4.2 now. That's simply the containment unit's normal ionic reading. It means the unit's EPM's singularity has been destroyed. That's why I'm stranded.

[Producer: So, why can't you create a new one?]

The singularity itself is created when the MTY device is docked on the collider floor. It takes a great deal of energy to form a singularity. An MTY device cannot form a singularity. If it could, I wouldn't be stranded. All the MTY device does is maintain and dilate the singularity once it has been created.

[Producer: What's that sound?]

That's the tunneling regulator spinning up. That's this unit here. It works with the tensor to re-position the singularity's event horizons at the proper quantum position. Without it, you might end up in the right time, but floating in space, or the wrong time, but in the right place.

[Associate Producer: I don't understand.]

Well... 12 hours ago, the Earth was in a different position in its orbit around the sun.

[Associate Producer: Ok.]

If you tried to transit from here to the same physical space you occupied 12 hours ago, you would find yourself floating in space.

[Associate Producer: I see.]

[Producer: What's the round thing?]

That's the EPM containment unit. It holds the micro singularity within a strong electromagnetic field.

[Associate Producer: What are those arms around it?]

Those are part of the tensor assembly. The tensor assembly calibrates or stabilizes a singularity. It also controls the singularity's spatial positioning, and the negative (P)Es exerted on the singularity's event horizon.

[Associate Producer: Event horizon?]

We call each side of the singularity an event horizon. Between the two event horizons is a timeless void. Time only exists outside of that void. When the two horizons are separated by spatial distance, that timeless void can be thought of as a tunnel through normal space-time. That's why quantum engineers call the mechanism that controls the door's spatial and quantum separation a "tunneling regulator".

The tensor's manipulation of the EPM field allows the two event horizons to be spatially-stabilized outside of the containment unit and dilated large enough for a person to enter and exit. At that point, we say the singularity has been calibrated.

For normal EPM transit, say between two cities, the two event horizons can be spatially-separated by thousands of kilometers, but they are still two sides of the same hole. When you enter one side, you exit the other side immediately.

For temporal tripback missions, the event horizons do not have any spatial-separation, but they do have quantum-separation.

The tensor assembly and the tunneling regulator work together. Once the singularity has been formed, the MTY's tensor assembly keeps one of the event horizons in current space-time, while the tunneling regulator allows the opposite event horizon to begin tunneling backward.

The tensor holds the singularity within an exotic phased matter field. The latitudinal arms along its surface of the EPM containment unit control that field strength.

[Associate Producer: I'm sorry. What is exotic… what did you call it?]

Exotic phased matter?

[Associate Producer: Yes.]

EPM is matter that is not composed of the subatomic particles of which ordinary matter is composed. The phased matter that we use in our MTY devices is composed of osmium ions, spinning at nearly the speed of light inside a QED vacuum chamber composed of electron-depleted osmium, and compressed by a very strong electromagnetic field.

In temporal engineering, we represent the dimensionless function as $\varsigma = T$ tens $-\varrho$ over $|\varrho|$, which we call the exoticity function. Now...

[Associate Producer: Hang on... hang on.]

[Producer: Yes. Um... you know what I'm thinking? I'm thinking we need to get... um... a mathematician... or a scientist in on this conversation.]

[Associate Producer: Yes. I agree. Um... I know someone we can call. **** ****. He's at ****.]

[Producer: Ok.]

[Associate Producer: I'll give him a call tonight.]

[Producer: Ok... Sounds good.]

The Mechanics of Time Travel

[Producer: So, let me ask you another question. The professor I spoke with about your email said it was not possible to use a wormhole to go back in time to a point before the wormhole existed.]

That's correct.

[Producer: Then how can you use a wormhole that you created in the future to come to our time now?]

I'll try to explain. A singularity, or wormhole to use your word, can be thought of as a spherical hole held in space-time by an energy force. The wormhole can be either microscopic or macroscopic. Very small or very large. Do you understand?

[Producer: I think so.]

When fully calibrated by the tensor assembly, the wormhole has two sides, a "near" and a "distant" event horizon. It resembles a true hole.

When you insert your finger into a hole, it is both entering on one side, and exiting on the other side simultaneously.

[Producer: Ok. I follow that.]

With a wormhole, however, the two sides of the hole can be spatially separated. If you were to place your arm through one side of a wormhole on earth, it would exit the other side of the wormhole at the same time, even if the other side of the wormhole was on Luna.

[*Producer: That's incredible!*]

[*Associate Producer: Amazing!*]

That's the principle of spatial separation.

Quantum separation, however, is an entirely different thing.

Once a singularity is formed... that is to say, once a wormhole is formed, the gravimetric force that created the wormhole begins to push it out of normal space-time. It actually starts pushing it backward in time at the same time it begins to self-annihilate.

This is what was happening in CERN's early collider experiments. Physicists at the time observed that the singularity would disappear the instant it was created. From this, they assumed that the singularity was unstable and had annihilated itself, but they were confused because it was leaving no supersymmetric particle tracks in their detectors.

They speculated that the absence of residual particle tracks was due to the singularity's gravitons escaping to some other dimension.

They were pretty close to being correct. The gravimetric force that forms a singularity begins pushing it, the singularity itself, into another dimension, that is to say, out of normal space-time. At the same time, the gravimetric force causes the singularity to self-annihilate.

The MTY's tensor assembly prevents that from happening. It keeps the wormhole in the present and it also prevents it from self-annihilating.

[*Producer: So, how do you go into the past?*]

The tunneling regulator interacts with the tensor assembly, causing it to release control of one of the wormhole's event horizons, what I like to call its "back door", to allow the gravimetric forces trying to push it out of normal space-time to succeed, but it keeps the other side, the front door, calibrated to the present.

When the back door reaches the desired quantum position, the tunneling regulator turns control back to the tensor assembly, which reduces the gravimetric force being applied to the back door, and re-stabilizes it in normal space-time again, but at an earlier quantum position; at an earlier point in time.

At that moment, the front door is in the current space-time, and the back door is perhaps 50 years earlier. Both doors still have a spatial separation of zero, but their quantum separation is now 50.

So, your professor friend is right. It's impossible to use a wormhole to transit to a time before the wormhole existed, but we can stabilize one of the wormhole's event horizons at an earlier point in time, while keeping its other event horizon at our present point in time, and then transit freely between those doors. At that moment, one of the wormhole's doors "existed" 50 years ago.

[Producer: Amazing!]

For normal EPM transit, say, between two cities, the two event horizons are calibrated spatially far apart, but are kept within the same point in time. They might have a spatial separation of 3,000 kilometers, but since they are both in the same space-time, their quantum separation is zero. Stepping through the hole take no time at all, even though its two doors are 3,000 kilometers apart.

For MTY tripbacks, the reverse is typically true; the spatial separation is zero, but the quantum separation might be 100 years.

[Associate Producer: But… it sounds like you can only open the door backward… I mean… to the past.]

That's correct.

[Associate Producer: So, how do you get back to the future?]

Once a specialist transits the event horizon, he switches the MTY's control unit into its holding cycle.

The front door… the event horizon that is still in the present, is suspended at that moment in time. The tunneling regulator eases the tensor assembly's front door EPM field, but very weakly this time. The front door is still not allowed to tunnel backward, but it no longer permitted to proceed forward in normal space-time either. It is suspended at that moment in time.

[Associate Producer: Ok.]

The event horizon that is in the past, however, the back door, is unlocked and permitted to proceed forward. This keeps the back door in sync with the specialist in the past.

[Associate Producer: I see.]

Once the front door is suspended, and the back door is moving forward in sync with the specialist, the tensor assembly decreases the EPM field strength dilating the singularity, shrinking it back to its microstate within the EPM containment unit.

[Associate Producer: So, how do you get back?]

When the specialist is ready to return, the control unit increases the EPM field strength against the singularity again, dilating it large enough to transit again. Then, the specialist simply steps back through the door, emerging at their original departure location as many seconds after they left as it took them in the past to place the EPM into its holding cycle. Usually, that takes only a few seconds.

[Associate Producer: I see.]

In my case, since I failed to return, RJCom and the CTI council representative would have had quantum engineers come to the site and scan for my singularity.

They would have discovered that my singularity had been destroyed, so, they undoubtedly retired my assignment marker and sent another specialist, who completed the mission the day before I had arrived.

[Producer: Does that happen often? I mean… someone getting stranded?]

No. It is very rare. In the 83 years we've had temporal singularities, I'm only the fourth specialist to be lost.

[Producer: Who were the others?]

Reynolds-Hampshire lost a specialist in 2114. He was the first. His name was Aleksei Lewis. He was lost in northern Kazakhstan in 1953. We don't know why he failed to return, but the speculation is that his MTY device's EPM field experienced particle disruption during the August 12 Semipalatinsk thermonuclear detonation he was sent to observe.

[Associate Producer: Do you know what happened to him?]

Not definitively.

In 1954, a French photographer named Henri Cartier-Bresson took a photograph in Moscow of two girls standing near an electric streetcar. NAFS archivists believe one of the men inside the streetcar is Lewis. The archive's SDUs report a 98.4% probability that it's Lewis.

[Associate Producer: What happened to the others?]

China reportedly lost a specialist in 2126, but they haven't released any details of the incident to the other CTI-certified nations.

RJCom lost a specialist, Theresa Williams, in 2137. I actually met Terri once, shortly after I was advanced to the Temporal Specialist Group at San Tibor. Her tripback file was sealed by the NAFS after she was lost, so I don't know what happened to her, but I know she had been sent to scan data files at the former USA Office of Personnel Management in the year 2015.

[Associate Producer: So, is there any limit on how far back someone can go?]

With enough power, an MTY's tunneling regulator could theoretically transit a person back to the point in time when matter was first formed, or 13.82 billion years ago. Of course, the amount of energy needed to transit back that far would approach the totality of the energy of the universe.

As a practical matter, we can transit back a couple hundred years with a reasonable energy cost.

[Associate Producer: Is that why we have not been visited by time travelers before now?]

That's correct. That is very astute.

Early quantum theorists such as Einstein and Hawking said time travel must not be possible, or man's early history would have been filled with accounts of time traveling tourists from the future.

Hawking even famously held a party for time travelers, and then did not send out the invitations until after the party had ended. Since no one had arrived at the earlier party, he said that was proof that time travel did not exist.

[Producer: Do you think someone would ever go back just to attend his party?]

Unlikely. Such a frivolous tripback would never be approved, but I will tell you that every few years, there is some group that lobbies for the CTI council to authorize a tripback for "Hawking's Party".

[Producer: That's hilarious!]

The reality, however, is that time travel requires an enormous amount of energy. The further back you wish to go, the more energy is required.

My parent's generation was the first to be able to generate enough power to transit time at all, and those early experiments were limited to tripbacks of only a few weeks or months.

With our current fusion reactors, we can generate sufficient power to transit back a couple hundred years, but the exponentially increasing power requirements make transiting further than that impossible.

My generation is the first to truly explore time, and while there are exceptions, the early to late modern age is about as far back as we can go.

There is a formula that temporal specialists use to approximate temporal tripback energy requirements, where P_E is the particle electron biteout of the EPM containment unit, t is the number of years you wish to transit, and e is the amount of energy in gigawatts required to calibrate to that time.

The formula is:

$$e = P_E(-(0.024t)^{5.7442}) + 98.507(P_E)$$

It's an approximate formula, of course. The actual calculations are so complex that they require a quantum-entangled analytic processor to compute.

RJCom's collider had to generate approximately 146 gigawatts of energy to form the singularity I used to transit to 2014.

[Associate Producer: So, we're never going to be visited by people from a thousand years in the future.]

Probably not. Given the correlation between temporal distance and energy cost, we believe it is extremely unlikely man will ever be able to transit backward more than five or six hundred years. Quantum statisticians believe that, even in the future, this power-to-time limitation will still exist.

To transit back 500 years, for example, would require more than 224 terawatts of power. That's almost twice the power the entire Earth produces... well, twice what it produces in my time.

So, we can't transit back thousands of years, and we can't expect to be visited by people from thousands of years in the future.

We are simply too temporally far removed from each other.

[Associate Producer: What's the furthest back we have traveled?]

Are you asking about me personally, or mankind?

[Associate Producer: Mankind.]

In 2119, about a year after I certed, Blosch Fusion announced it had partnered with Nishikawa Manufacturing. Blosch had just completed construction of its UHP 7TW-Fusion reactor in Norway, and they wanted to demonstrate its capabilities. They also wanted to enter the singularity market.

So, they partnered with Nishikawa, who manufactured EPM containment units and tensor assembly controllers. The company began manufacturing its own EPM transit devices, and they submitted their own MTY device design to the CTI council, to compete with RJCom and Reynolds-Hampshire.

Britain's Office of Temporal Affairs wanted to scan a collection of early daguerreotypes on display at the 1851 Great Exhibition in London. That was 268 years back. Until then, the energy limits of even the largest fusion reactors prevented such a distant tripback mission.

So, Blosch-Nishikawa obtained permission from the CTI council in Geneva to complete the request.

I remember scanning it about a year after I had started at Tout-Su. It took 6.1 terawatts of energy just to calibrate that singularity, and more than 560 gigawatts to maintain it. Their MTY device was fitted with the largest portable fusion reactor available. I heard that the specialist could barely lift the device and that it took more than 30 minutes to calibrate. That was the furthest tripback mission man has yet accomplished.

[Producer: How do you remember all that information… the dates, and power levels, and things like that?]

I don't actually. Most of it I receive from my datstem. I have always had a personal interest in quantum engineering and history, but most of the details are provided by my datstem.

[Associate Producer: So, how does that work? Are you reading some kind of screen in your head?]

No. I don't have any ocular implants. I never liked the idea of data obstructing my view, and I've always thought that the people who get them look strange, staring like they do.

HOW TO BUILD A TIME MACHINE

[Associate Producer: So, how does it work?]

A datstem is a sophisticated quantum-entangled computing and analytic processor. It has vast data storage, as well as extremely fast algorithmic and rational processing capabilities. It's what you people would call "artificial intelligence".

It's like having a thought come into your head. You can tell it's coming from your datstem, and you can disregard it or even turn the unit off if you wish. Your mind gets used to the influx of information, and actually gets trained to sort it out it in a very short time. Essentially, it is listening to our conversation and supplies me with information it determines would be relevant.

[Producer: Jesus.]

[Associate Producer: Yeah. I think I'm going to take away my daughter's smartphone when I get home!]

A datstem is actually one of the ways to identify a temporal specialist in the past. It's why a temporal specialist is never observed using period-typical electronic data devices.

[Producer: besides knowledge… I mean… what else can it do? For example, can you use it to speak a foreign language?]

Actually yes, but only if you acquire a linguistic interface upgrade. I actually acquired a Japanese linguistic upgrade 10 years ago for a tripback I made to the 2003 International Robot Exposition in Tokyo, Japan.

[Producer: So, you can just speak Japanese whenever you want?]

はい. 私は防府駅にアパートがあるので便利です.

[Producer: Amazing.]

[Associate Producer: So... um... how long does it take? I mean... for the person who is going back through time?]

It takes no time to traverse the event horizon itself. You step through and you're when you wanted to be. But it does take time for the tunneling regulator to achieve temporal calibration, based on the quantum date entered into the control unit.

It takes RJCom's tunneling regulators 3.7 seconds for each year of time being traversed. The ones manufactured by Blosch-Nishikawa calibrate faster, at 2.5 seconds per year, but they have a wider short-range calibration cycle. That is, they cannot quantum-lock to close dates as precisely as RJCom's, but they have a comparable distant quantum-lock.

It took my RJCom MTY device approximately 8 minutes to calibrate the EPM singularity for me to transit to 2014.

[Producer: What year did you come from?]

2151.

A Discussion on Temporal Causality

[Associate Producer: I'm sorry, but I need to ask a question.]

Yes?

[Associate Producer: By telling us all of this, aren't you changing the future or something? I mean…]

** Laughing **

[Associate Producer: What?... I mean… aren't you… um…]

I apologize for laughing, but the people here all believe time travel can't be possible because, if it were, time travelers would create universe-destroying paradoxes.

[Associate Producer: Right.]

I do not mean to denigrate, but that theory was disproved long ago.

One of the things we discovered about time is that causal-loop-paradoxes cannot occur.

The Luyteni 9th signal series provided us with theoretical and technical information that allowed us to dismiss causality...

[Associate Producer: I'm sorry. Lou-teny?]

Ah… Yes.

In the year 2046, mankind received a response to a radio signal sent in 2017 from the city of Tromsø Norway to Luyten's

Star. That's star GJ-273. It's a red dwarf system located approximately 12.4 light-years from Earth.

[Producer: A response? You mean... from another planet?]

Yes.

[Producer: Jesus!]

[Associate Producer: Holy shit!]

Their subsequent TVS pulse signals contained information that...

[Associate Producer: TVS?]

A TVS pulse is a time-varying spectra pulse. Basically, they are light pulses with time separations of the order of 10^{-9} to 10^{-15} s that can be detected against the visible spectra of a star.

In 2046, the PARAS spectrograph at Mount Abu, India detected a repeating series of 22 pulse sequences against the background spectra of Luyten's star.

After 2 years, the pulses were decrypted. We discovered that the signals were transmitted from a technically advanced civilization in the Luyten star system who had received our early Tromsø signal.

The sequences contained...

[Associate Producer: Do they visit the earth? Um... I mean... have you seen them?]

No. We can't visit their planet and they can't visit ours... at least... not yet.

[Associate Producer: Too far?]

That's correct.

An MTY's singularity is held within a phased matter field. The phased matter itself is quantum entangled. So, while an MTY's tunneling regulator can calibrate a singularity event horizon to different points in time, the physical distance between the singularity's event horizons... between its front door and its back door, is restricted by the maximum distance possible between quantum-entangled particles.

Entangled particles are disrupted by collisions with ordinary atoms. The furthest spatial distance we can transit between areas of dense matter, say, through the earth, is approximately 28,000 kilometers.

We can transit through empty space up to 2.3 million kilometers. Of course, space isn't really empty. If it were, we'd be able to transit much further.

We understand the Luyteni have stabilized their singularities as far as 21.4 million kilometers. But that's still only an infinitesimal fraction of the distance between our two star systems.

We'd have to construct more than 51 million singularly platforms to even reach the Luyten star system. And even if we could, and even if it only took 1 second to transit each singularity, it would still take us 1.6 years to get there.

So, no. We can't visit them, and they can't visit us. Until we solve the particle collision problem, we can't visit each other.

[Associate Producer: I see.]

That's one reason why temporal specialists must wait until the planet's orbital position is as close as possible to what it was during the target time, and why they are transported as close as possible to their target destination. It reduces atomic disruption on the singularity's entangled phased-matter field. When my tripback was approved by the CTI counsel, I had to wait almost four months before I was cleared to proceed.

We can transit to any place on the planet. People routinely transit to the moon, to the orbital stations, even to the colonies on Mars, though it's expensive and you have to transit through numerous EPM platforms to get there.

If you lose a singularity on a transit platform, say, when you're on your way to a far-orbital station, you might be stranded for a few minutes, until a new singularity is calibrated.

But if you lose a singularity when you're on a tripback mission... well, that's it. You're stranded in that time because of the gen-lock limiters on MTY devices.

So, as a matter of policy, temporal specialists are transported as close as possible to their destination coordinates before transitioning, to minimize any particle collision.

[Associate Producer: Ok, but why can't paradoxes happen?]

Self-resolving causality prevents it.

[Associate Producer: What about the whole... if I kill my grandfather in the past thing... I mean... how can I be born if...]

Yes. I understand what you are asking. That's the classic

causality loop paradox, but that theory was disproved long ago. Well… from my point of view, it was long ago.

Any event that might cause a paradox self-resolves in such a way that no paradox can occur.

[Associate Producer: I don't understand.]

Causality loop theory says if you transited back in time and killed your grandfather before he had any children, since your actions would result in you never having been born, then you cannot have transited back in time to kill your grandfather. Hence, a paradox.

[Associate Producer: Right!]

But, in fact, if you were to go back in time and kill your grandfather, the man you killed could not be your grandfather.

[Associate Producer: That doesn't make sense.]

What we discovered was, if an action could cause a paradox in the past, then the probability of that action is zero. Time "self-resolves" to prevent paradoxes from occurring.

This is not a new concept. It used to be called the "Novikov" or "self-consistency" principle, but now we simply call it "self-resolving causality".

[Associate Producer: I guess I just don't understand…]

It's impossible for a temporal specialist to do something in the past that would change the future from which they came…

up to the point in time from which they transited to the past. The laws of temporal mechanics prevent it.

Specifically, for any quantum system in a singularity space-time that has a stable event horizon, all of the possible outcomes of one's actions are self-consistent, or self-resolving.

What that means is, when a person has traveled back in time, using a singularity with a stable event horizon, they cannot do anything in the past that can change the shape of time that exists on the other side of that event horizon... at least up to the point in time from which they came.

Einstein, Eddington, Hawking, and Penrose all understood the concept of a paradox but they incorrectly concluded that time travel must not be possible because universe-shattering paradoxes had not occurred.

They didn't consider the possibility that time resolves paradoxes; that the infinite number of possible changes to the past, might spawn an infinite number of self-correcting resolutions to keep time consistent.

[Associate Producer: So, the future can't be changed by anything you do in the past.]

Precisely.

Some early physicists studying the Luyteni equations thought that this meant a time traveler would not be able to exercise free will while they were in the past. They believed any person who went through a singularity would be prevented by physical laws from making changes to the past.

That is both true, and yet not true.

What we discovered is that a person can exercise free will and do anything they wish in the past, and the number of possible outcomes to those actions are infinite, but all of those possible outcomes self-resolve to prevent changes to the future from which they came.

So, a temporal specialist has free will to do what they wish, but nothing they do can alter the future from which they came. For anything they do that might cause a paradox, time will cause a negation… a resolution of their actions. Time will resolve itself to prevent an action from affecting the future, up to the point in time from which they left.

Using your grandfather analogy, a person in the past could pull the trigger and the gun might misfire. Or they might kill the man only to later discover he wasn't their grandfather. The possibilities are infinite. But no matter what the time traveler does, it cannot change the future from which he came. Time will resolve his actions to maintain the future that sent him into the past.

Quantum theorists in my time have actually tried to conceive of a paradox that cannot be resolved, but they couldn't. The possible outcomes are infinite, so the possible resolutions are equally infinite.

[Associate Producer: That's very confusing.]

I agree.

What is even more confusing is when you understand that, while a person in the past cannot affect the future from which they came, that limitation only applies to those events that occurred up to the point in time from which they transited to the past.

Their actions in the past can indeed alter their future's future, meaning, the time after the point when they transited to the past.

[Associate Producer: How?]

Well… consider this. The purpose of my own tripback mission was to retrieve information from the past, information that would be read and discussed by archivists and specialists at a point in time after I had transited to the past. Their actions will undoubtedly be influenced by that information.

So, while my actions in the past cannot affect the future up to the point I left, it will affect what occurs after that. It will affect my future's future.

[Associate Producer: This makes my head spin.]

Quantum mechanics can be very confusing if you aren't trained to it. The important point is, nothing I say or do here can change the future, up to that point from which I left. My awareness of that future, while I am here in the past, validates, or proves that future. "Knowledge makes the future real" is a common expression from my time, which is something people say when explaining self-resolving causality.

Unfortunately for me, self-resolving causality is the reason why I cannot expect to be rescued. The CTI council knows nothing a temporal specialist does in the past can significantly affect the future. The CTI council would actually risk more attempting to rescue me than to simply retire my assignment marker.

I don't blame them. It's the risk I accepted when I joined the San Tibor group, but it is frustrating.

I want to share what I know with the world, to try and help

mankind take a step forward, but ultimately, I know it won't alter the future… at least up to the point I left.

Oh, it might change the shape of those immediate events that create that future, but in the end, the future itself will not be changed.

So… as I said in my earlier communication, I'm choosing to share this information because I don't want to simply disappear, forgotten, and abandoned. No other motive is possible for me. Perhaps that's a selfish reason. I'm not sure, but I do hope that something I do or say will be meaningful in some way to the future. If not to the future, then perhaps to the future's future.

[Producer: Ok...um… Look… I think we should take a break.]

[Producer's note: we took an approximate 90-minute lunch break in the hotel room.]

John J. Clifton

[Producer: Ok...I'm recording again. So... um... we talked at lunch about setting up a meeting with some people who can understand the mathematics and science you are talking about. So, for now, could you please share some information about yourself, about your mission... I mean, why are you here?]

Where should I begin?

[Producer: Why don't you start with an introduction?]

An introduction?

[Producer: Yes. We didn't get that recorded yet. Tell us about yourself, and about your mission. You just talk and we'll try not to interrupt.]

Very well.

My name is John J. Clifton. I was born in 2100, 27 years after the Resettlement Ban was lifted that allowed relocation back into the western part of the North America Federated States.

I was born in New Phoenix, near what people here call Phoenix, Arizona.

After the American Conflict ended in 2042, the western region of the former United States was heavily contaminated with cesium 137. The region was quarantined and resettlement prohibited until 2073 when the ban was lifted.

My grandmother was a radiological specialist and was one of the first women approved for resettlement. She moved to the Hohokam region in 2074, to a camp called "Hohokam Station

4". She met my grandfather there. He was a heavy equipment operator assigned to the camp's salvage and reclamation units.

My mother was born in 2077 at Station 4 before the camp was closed. After my mother completed her primary instruction, she trained in genomic modeling and accepted an assignment at a yī-yuàn facility in New Phoenix…

[Producer: I'm sorry. I didn't get that… Yee wan?]

A yī-yuàn… a medical facility.

[Producer: Is that like a hospital?]

Yes. A hospital.

[Producer: I see.]

My father was a power engineer at Smith Solar Cooperative in New Phoenix. He met my mother when he was injured repairing a long wave distributor and was transported to the yī-yuàn… to the hospital, where my mother was assigned.

I was born in New Phoenix in 2100. I received my primary instruction at Rio Verde Primary where I certed in mathematics, continental history, and temporal engineering. I was advanced twice, so I began my secondary instruction early.

I was certed in secondary temporal engineering in 2126 and was assigned to the generation team at Tout-Su Particles in New Phoenix.

After five years, I submitted a reassignment marker, which was acquired by Rengel-Jiang QCom. I was assigned to their research facility at San Tibor in Texas, approximately 90 kilometers west of today's Houston Texas.

In 2137 I was advanced to the Temporal Specialist Group at San Tibor.

In the 14 years since then, I have completed 11 tripbacks, including the one 4 years ago that left me stranded here.

[Producer: How did you get stranded?]

I was sent by RJCom to retrieve a data file from an electrical power generation facility located in Austin, Texas in the year 2014. The file was known to contain a list of the energy subscribers in the Austin region at that time.

RJCom was trying to locate the property coordinates of a man named Barrett, whose family was known to have owned property in the Austin area in 2014.

[Producer: Why?]

When the American Conflict began in 2041, Barrett had been attached to UCF Houston ComHQ in Texas and assigned to its regional staff in Austin. When the UCF began its Gulf Retreat in December 2041, Barrett reportedly buried ComHQ strategic records somewhere "on his family's property in Austin".

It is hoped that those UCF documents will identify the location of any nuclear mines buried and forgotten by the retreating UCF forces. One such mine was recently unearthed by a construction crew in Burnet, Texas. It detonated, killing more than 42,000 people.

[Producer: Jesus!]

After the Burnet disaster, Texas received funding from the NAFS and authorization from the CTI council for a tripback mission.

My tripback was to scan the power facility's customer data file in the year 2014 and return it to RJCom. This would allow NAFS archival teams to identify the coordinates of Barrett's family property near Austin. They hope to locate the UCF Houston ComHQ records reportedly concealed by Barrett on the property, and then use those records to locate any other forgotten nuclear mines.

After my mission briefing, I was gen-locked to my MTY device, CTI gave me final clearance, and RJCom's med techs administered a standard neustem injection.

[Associate Producer: I'm sorry…What exactly is 'new stem'? You mentioned that before.]

A neustem is a biomechanical implant designed for inhibitor and neuro conditioning. All temporal specialists are required to receive a neustem implant. It's implanted near the brain stem… about here… can you see this?

[Associate Producer: the bump?]

Yes. That's my neustem's injection pod. It ports to my neustem implant.

Neustem implants release gen-coded biochems into the brain that inhibit the specialist from disclosing mission information. They prevent a temporal specialist from… well… from doing what I am doing right now… telling you about the future.

[Associate Producer: Your email said yours had worn off?]

Yes. Neustem biochems deplete naturally over time if they're not immediately countered at the post-mission briefing.

[Associate Producer: Ok.]

After receiving my MTY device and neustem injection, I performed two verifications of my device's EPM before I was transported to the site location. That's protocol.

I checked the tensor after I calibrated the MTY on RJCom's collider floor. It read negative .144 (P)Es.

I checked it again while we were waiting for the transport to arrive. The tensor read negative .152 (P)Es.

Both readings were logged by CentralDat and witnessed by the CTI council representative present, so I'm certain that there was no failure of the EPM containment unit before on-site transit.

My RJCom administrator and the CTI representative accompanied me in the transport to the site location inside of Austin. Once there, I set the MTY's control unit to March 13, 2014, 00:05 local time and initiated the EPM dilation. I then traversed the singularity without incident.

Upon arrival, I immediately set the MTY to its holding cycle and concealed the device in the pack I was provided. I remember glancing at the tensor before placing it in the pack, and it was reading negative .151 (P)Es, so I know the singularity was still stable after my arrival.

I proceeded towards a large gathering I had scanned at my mission briefing to be a local music festival. I could see the lights and hear the music from my arrival location. I intended to lose myself in the crowd in the event my arrival had been observed.

I was walking with groups of people on Red River transway towards the music when something struck me violently from behind. I estimate I was thrown approximately 4 meters and lost consciousness upon impact with the surface.

[Producer: You were hit by a car?]

Yes. I scanned later that an intoxicated transport operator had struck me and numerous other people while attempting to elude local authorities.

When I regained consciousness, I was in considerable discomfort. There were a number of medical transports on the street attending to injured people. Several people were attempting to assist me, telling me not to move, but they had not removed my pack.

When I tried to stand, I discovered that my left arm was fractured. I also had two cracked ribs and assorted bruising. The discomfort was considerable, even through my neustem.

In accordance with temporal protocols, I immediately returned to my arrival point and attempted to dilate the EPM to return.

When the EPM failed to dilate, I performed a preliminary visual inspection of the containment unit. I could not observe any damage to the unit, but the control unit tensor display registered positive, so I knew even then that the singularity must have been destroyed.

I was in considerable discomfort so I made my way back into the city and located a yī-yuàn facility. I was injected with a morphine-based pain suppressant and subjected to what appeared to be a radiographic scan of my arm and chest. Later, a med tech encased my injured arm in a glass fiber reinforced polymer cloth, which rendered it completely immobile.

When I was released later that morning, I hired a transport who delivered me to a hotel in the city proximal to the power facility. After securing my room, I was able to perform a more thorough examination of the MTY device and its EPM containment unit, where I discovered the microfracture I mentioned in my earlier communication.

I gained entry into one the power facility's ancillary support buildings that evening. After accessing the target file system with my PoL device, I discovered an RJCom tagdat sequence in the base directory. I knew then that my mission had been chong-fu'd.

[Producer: "Chon few"?]

I apologize. That's sino-slang. It means the mission was completed by another specialist.

[Associate Producer: And what is a "tag dat" sequence?]

A tagdat is simply a numerical sequence left within an electronic file when a temporal specialist completes a data retrieval mission during an information age tripback. It can inform other specialists that the data has been retrieved, but its primary purpose is to assist NAFS Archives in our time with locating tagged data in the event the files were ever archived.

[Associate Producer: Look... I still don't understand why they

couldn't just send someone back for you?]

My MTY's singularity has been destroyed.

[Associate Producer: I don't understand. Why can't they just open another wormhole for you, or send someone back with another device for you to use?]

Ah. I understand.

After the first temporal transit was achieved in 2068, an international treaty was passed requiring all tripbacks… all temporal missions, to be authorized by the CTI council. All MTY-capable nations subscribe to the treaty.

Under that treaty, all MTY devices are manufactured with a gen-lock that is synchronized with the operating specialist's neustem-QK signature during calibration.

This prevents people in the past from, say, killing a specialist, and using their MTY device. It also prevents a specialist from bringing someone from the past into the future, which is prohibited under the same treaty.

Essentially, an MTY device will only permit someone to transit whose neustem-QK signature matches the singularity's (P)E calibration.

So, even if they sent someone on a tripback just for me, I can't use their singularity to return.

[Associate Producer: I see.]

Once my singularity was destroyed, I was stranded.

[Associate Producer: I understand.]

[Producer: Ok. Look… here's what I want to do. We're going to set up a meeting with some people…   like we discussed. Probably a mathematician, and… ****, did you say that **** **** is a physicist?]

[Associate Producer: Yes. He's teaching at **** right now. He'd be a good place to start.]

[Producer: Ok. So… um… we should call him right away. In the meantime, can you get those history files to us that we talked about? The files about the war and the Luyteni, and the other things we talked about at lunch?]

Certainly. I cataloged the topics while we shared our meal. Should I transmit the files to the same communication address that I used earlier?

[Producer: Actually… no. I think we should keep this off the company's email server. Send it to ********@*******. Ok?]

I understand.

[Producer: Do you need to write it down?]

No. I've scanned it. One moment.

The files have been transmitted.

[Associate Producer: How did you do that?]

There are 1,633 distinct transmission nodes within range of

my datstem implant at this time.

My datstem identified 62 electronic communications that were actively transmitting at that moment and simply streamed the files behind one of the communications to a primary node.

It then redirected the file stream as a separate communication through several relay points to the recipient address you provided.

[Producer: I just got it! Incredible! Ok... So...We're going to arrange another interview with some people. Like... a mathematician, or a scientist, or some people like that...]

I understand.

[Producer: Great. Ok... I'm going to stop recording now.]

Producer's note: The following summary files were received on January 26th, 2018 attached to an email communication sent by Mr. Clifton to our executive producer's personal email address. The files covered a number of topics about which more information had been requested by our producers.

The American Conflict

Begin Summary File: EF8FAD856//:QKDS-51676F54A

Background and Contributing Factors

The American Conflict (2041 – 2042) was a civil war fought within the geographic boundaries of the (former) United States of America (USA), eastern Canada, and the northern Mexican states.

As early as the 1960s, the civic and political climate of the USA had begun to coalesce into two competing socio-economic models; capitalism and socialism.

Throughout the 1980s and 1990s, proponents of each model became increasingly activist in nature, and by the year 2000, the two largest political parties of the time, Republicans and Democrats, began to align against each other along these socio-economic lines; Republicans to capitalism, and Democrats to socialism.

During the Obama presidency (2009 – 2017), hostilities between the two groups dramatically increased, fueled by the policies of the Obama administration that supported socialist programs.

Following the election of Donald Trump in 2017, democratic political leaders who had enjoyed years of unrestrained support for socialist programs under the Obama presidency felt threatened and disenfranchised. Despite economic, civic, and international achievements during the Trump presidency, democratic party leaders refused to support the Trump administration. Encouraged by leftist media sources and popular celebrities, socialist leaders within the country became increasingly intransigent and hostile, further polarizing the democratic party's political base.

Throughout the 2020s "democratic socialist" marches were held in Seattle, Portland Oregon, San Francisco, Boston, and New York City; the latter attended by more than a million people.

In early 2030, the mayor of San Francisco declared the city to be a "socialist sanctuary" and "open to all who embrace socialist ideals". Before the year's end, more than 630,000 undocumented foreign nationals had migrated to the city.

The 2030s was marred by violence as democratic socialists began employing increasingly extremist methods to achieve their political objectives.

A series of car bombs in 2034 and 2035 killed or injured 16 conservative lawmakers across the nation before the perpetrators were caught.

In October 2035, Governor Hoffman of Arkansas, a vocal critic of the democratic party's "immigrant first, American second" policy, was assassinated on the steps of the Arkansas capital building.

In January 2036, a mob of leftist students, accompanied by hundreds of undocumented foreign nationals, and urged on by 3 socialist professors, attacked a group of conservative Republican students marching in support of free speech at the University of California at Berkeley, killing 8 of the students.

Campus violence against conservative students and educators continued to escalate throughout 2036, resulting in the forced closure of 5 public universities across the nation.

In May 2037, after signing into law a bill making it a felony to disrupt free speech events at state-funded schools and other state properties, Governor Cardon of Arizona, his wife, and 3 of their 4 children were brutally murdered in their home.

In October 2038, 14 armed men seized control of an elementary school in Stinnett, Texas, holding the students and staff hostage, and demanding the release of four compatriots arrested the previous month for assassinating an outspoken Republican state lawmaker. When 3 days of negotiations failed, the men began shooting their hostages, killing 74 children and 22 teachers before national guardsmen retook the campus.

After similar attacks in 2039 against elementary schools in Texas, Georgia, North Carolina, and Florida, on November 9, 2039, the president ordered federal troops across the nation to assume active duty guard positions at all of the nation's public schools. More than 630 public schools closed their doors, rather than continue to endanger their students.

On May 1, 2040, while speaking to a group of labor activists assembled in Seattle, Washington, Vice President Shapiro, the Republican party candidate in the upcoming presidential election, was shot and killed by Luis Cadenas, a 43-year old Venezuelan undocumented foreign national.

The following day, on May 2, 2040, Democratic Party Committee leaders published a statement, openly praising the assassination, labeling the murdered candidate a "racist", and urging party members to continue to resist the "capitalist oligarchs". The party also announced a formal name change to the Democratic Socialist Party of America.

Two days later, on May 4, 2040, while en-route to attend the slain candidate's memorial service, the president's transport was attacked by small arms fire from a pursuing transport. A rocket-propelled grenade struck the rear of the president's transport, killing the president and a security officer. The first lady and the transport operator were critically injured.

Federal security agents engaged the attackers, killing three and capturing a fourth, all members of a militant democratic socialist group.

Following the attack, suspicion immediately fell on leaders within the Democratic Socialist Party Committee. When the sole surviving attacker later confessed to having received funding and support for the attack from the committee through a Venezuelan intermediary with close ties to Cadenas, rioting broke out across the nation.

On June 3, 2040, claiming authority under then USA Title 47 U.S. Code § 606, and citing the nationwide rioting as their justification, democratic members of the House of Representatives, then in the majority, passed the infamous Electoral Suspension Act of 2040. The Act suspended the upcoming presidential elections and named the Speaker of the House (and Democratic Socialist Committee chair) as President.

Outraged Republican house members walked out en-masse, calling the Act unconstitutional, and the assassinations nothing less than a coup d'état.

The Senate adjourned and formally dissolved the following day.

Violence across the nation increased over the next five months, as state governors struggled to assume operational control of federal resources and mobilize state national guard units.

On November 2, 2040, the date previously scheduled for the presidential election, the governor of California issued an expulsion order, calling for the forced removal of all federal troops from the state. When state guardsmen attempted to forcibly expel federal troops from the San Jose and San Bruno armories, fighting erupted, resulting in 82 federal troops and 113 state guardsmen dead.

Throughout the waning days of 2040, tensions continued to escalate as military forces gathered under local state governors, and civilian populations began relocating along ideological lines to politically-sympathetic states.

On January 1, 2041, Republican congressional representatives announced they had established a constitutional legislative body at Ft. Bragg, North Carolina *(See: "The Ft. Bragg Congress: Provisional Government During the American Conflict"; NAFS-Archive Unit 09, 3s - (ar) 2082, Summary File: F3DB465885).*

Under the authority of the Ft. Bragg Congress, regional military and administrative headquarters were established in Houston (Texas), Dugway Proving Ground (Utah), Ft. Bragg (North Carolina), Carlisle Army Base (Pennsylvania), and Ft. Benning (Georgia).

On February 11, 2041, California, Connecticut, Delaware, Hawaii, Oregon, Maine, Massachusetts, New Hampshire, New Jersey, New York, Rhode Island, Vermont, and Washington state formally announced their secession from the USA as the Independent Socialist States of America (ISSA).

The Ft. Bragg Congress responded swiftly, condemning the announcement and refusing to recognize ISSA. United States armed forces loyal to the Ft. Bragg Congress were re-named United Capitalist Forces (UCF) and immediately ordered north and west.

Historians consider the ISSA secession declaration on February 11, 2041, to be the start of the American Conflict.

Battle of Worcester

The first military engagement between the opposing sides took place on March 17, 2041, between UCF Carlisle Armor Group 4 and elements of ISSA's Atlantic Command, then occupying New York state.

UCF Carlisle ComHQ in Pennsylvania ordered its Armor Group 4 to proceed north towards Schenectady, New York. Their objective was to attempt to draw ISSA forces into central New York state and then move swiftly southeast to capture or destroy the ordnance manufacturing facilities at ISSA's Watervliet Arsenal.

In the early morning hours of March 17, 2041, a UCF remote combat vehicle (RCV) attached to Armor Group 4 was intercepted by ISSA forces outside of the small town of Worcester, New York. The RCV fired two anti-tank missiles, destroying an advancing ISSA AP-Squad Carrier vehicle before it was itself destroyed. Before being destroyed, however, the RCV transmitted images showing ISSA forces staging east of the town.

28 M1A9 Abrams Tanks from UCF Armor Group 4 advanced, taking up positions 6 kilometers to the west of the town, straddling the old interstate transway. The heavy, slow-moving armor was supported by 7 SHORAD short-range air defense Stryker vehicles, 4,200 UCF troops, and 18 MPF Mobile-Protected Firepower light tanks swiftly airlifted to the area from Carlisle ComHQ.

At approximately 11:15, ISSA forces attacked, deploying 10 S-97 Raider attack helicopters to engage the UCF armor. While the Raiders were engaging the tanks, nearly 14,000 ISSA troops supported by 32 MPFs advanced from their staging area east of the town.

The S-97 Raiders destroyed 8 of the UCF M1A9 Abrams heavy tanks before UCF commanders committed their SHORAD Strykers, destroying the attacking Raiders.

Now without air support, ISSA forces attempted to bring their MPFs within range of the UCF Abrams tanks, but the lighter MPFs could not penetrate the heavier Abrams' reactive armor.

Figure 1 - M1A9 Abrams tank attached to UCF Armor Group 4 firing on ISSA forces at Battle of Worcester, March 17, 2041. Image courtesy Scherer American Conflict Museum, Pittsburgh PA, NAFS. File Number 0103G.

Despite their nearly 3 to 1 numerical superiority, by noon, the ISSA forces began retreating back through Worcester. Rather than risk losing their remaining MPFs to the advancing Abrams, ISSA commanders directed the surviving MPFs to retreat ahead of their forces.

Observing the maneuver, UCF MPFs swiftly advanced, flanking the remaining ISSA forces southwest of the town, and cutting off their retreat. Threatened by the Abrams tanks advancing from their rear, and flanked by the fast-moving MPFs ahead, the trapped ISSA forces surrendered.

Casualties and Assessment

UCF losses were 10 M1A9 Abrams tanks, 6 MPFs, and 1 RCV destroyed. 847 troops were killed, wounded, or captured.

ISSA losses were 10 S-97 Raiders and 14 MPFs destroyed. 3,881 troops were killed, wounded, or captured.

Though the losses on both sides were insignificant by later Conflict standards, the battle represented a blow to ISSA morale and emboldened UCF forces across the nation.

ISSA Central Committee Objectives

After its defeat at the Battle of Worcester, ISSA Central Committee leaders in San Francisco, California were determined to bring a swift end to the conflict.

Coordinating with its leadership in the east, the ISSA Central Committee's strategy was to launch a coordinated three-pronged thrust, from the east, north-west, and west, and force the Ft. Bragg Congress to either surrender or recognize ISSA sovereignty.

ISSA Atlantic Command forces would move swiftly south from New York, Delaware, and Maryland, launch an air strike against the UCF-held Norfolk Naval Base in Virginia and then push on into North Carolina to threaten or possibly capture the Ft. Bragg Congress.

At the same time, ISSA North-Western Command forces would push east from its bases in Seattle and Portland, capture Mountain Home Air Force Base in Idaho, and then push south into Nevada and Utah. An ISSA air strike group, launched from Mountain Home AFB, would destroy UCAF Hill Air Force Base in Utah, while North-Western Command forces captured UCF Dugway ComHQ.

While ISSA forces were attacking from the east and the north-west, ISSA Western Command forces would launch a massive two-pronged attack from California, pushing east through Arizona, New Mexico, and into Texas, with the goal of defeating UCF Houston ComHQ.

Clandestine ISSA Objectives

Dugway Proving Grounds, located approximately 130 km southwest of Salt Lake City, Utah, was the primary testing site for the former USA's chemical, biological, and nuclear weapons program.

Pursuant to international treaties signed in 1997 at the Chemical Weapons Convention in Hague, all chemical weapons stockpiles within the former USA had been destroyed by 2023.

Following the outbreak of hostilities at the Battle of Worcester, representatives of ISSA and the Ft. Bragg Congress signed the International Agreement of the American Combatants (IAAC), in Ottawa, Canada.

While the use of chemical, biological, or nuclear weapons had been expressly disclaimed by both sides under the IAAC, the ISSA Central Committee intended to seize the research and development facilities at Dugway and, if its military efforts failed, use the threat of chemical or biological attack to force the Ft. Bragg Congress to capitulate.

Battle of Norfolk

After the Battle of Worcester in March of 2041, heavy armor units from ISSA Eastern Command began deploying south from New York into northern Pennsylvania. At the same time, ISSA Atlantic Command forces began quietly moving ground and light armor units south through New Jersey and Delaware into Maryland.

ISSA regional commanders hoped to draw forces away from UCF Carlisle ComHQ and UCF Ft. Bragg ComHQ north into Pennsylvania. Once the UCF units were diverted, ISSA Atlantic Command would then push swiftly south from Maryland into Virginia's Eastern Shore region and cross the Chesapeake Bay to Norfolk Virginia.

ISSA special forces units would destroy the UCF communication facilities at the Joint Expeditionary Base – Little Creek, while an ISSA air strike group attacked the UCF fleet at Norfolk Naval Station.

Following the destruction of the UCF naval forces at Norfolk, the ISSA Atlantic Command forces would then push south into North Carolina, with the goal of capturing the Ft. Bragg Congress and forcing a swift end to the conflict.

Raid on Joint Expeditionary Base – Little Creek

On the evening of April 10, 2041, ISSA Atlantic Command launched 44 Defiant and 43 aging V-22 Osprey transport helicopters, supported by 22 S-97 Raider attack helicopters, from staging areas near Westover, Maryland. The aircraft proceeded covertly south through the Chesapeake Bay and landed 1100 commandos at Chic's Beach, approximately two kilometers east of the Joint Expeditionary Base – Little Creek.

At the same time, ISSA Atlantic Command ground forces, now totaling more than 160,000 troops, and supported by more than 1,400 pieces of light armor, began moving swiftly from their assembly areas in southern Maryland into Virginia's Eastern Shore region.

The light armored units consisted primarily of MPF mobile protected firepower light tanks, RCV remote combat vehicles, SHORAD short-range air defense Strykers, AMPV armored multi-purpose vehicles, DSLP drone swarming launch platforms, A-DEW avenger-series directed energy weapons, and THAAD terminal high-altitude air defense platforms.

In addition to its light armor and air-defense units, the force also fielded approximately 650 artillery pieces, primarily M142 HIMARS rocket launchers, M109A6 155mm Paladin self-propelled howitzers, and M1129 mortar-carrier Strykers.

In the early morning hours of April 11, 2041, the ISSA commandos, supported by their S-97 Raider attack helicopters, attacked the UCF garrison at Joint Expeditionary Base – Little Creek. The commandos swiftly destroyed the base's communications building and ancillary towers, while the Raiders began attacking the 20 SSC and LCAC hovercraft at the base docks.

The base garrison, consisting of approximately 23,000 UCF troops, advisors, and civilian personnel, engaged the heavily-armed attackers in bloody building-to-building fighting. After nearly an hour, the commandos inexplicably withdrew and entrenched themselves east of Lake Bradford.

When the pursuing UCF troops approached, however, they were shocked to discover light armor units of ISSA Atlantic Command assembled in force, with thousands of troops deploying into Bayside from the Chesapeake Bay Bridge.

Air Strike on Norfolk Naval Station

When the ISSA commandos began their attack on the Joint Expeditionary Base, UCF LCdr Christopher Devon, the duty officer at the NCTAMS communications building at the nearby Norfolk Naval Station, observed smoke rising from the direction of the base. Despite having received no word of an attack in progress, Devon immediately transmitted an emergency sortie signal to the 67 UCF warships then in port.

Figure 2 - UCF warships on fire in Hampton Roads, Battle of Norfolk, April 11, 2041. Image courtesy Norfolk Naval Station Archive.

Due to his quick thinking, 63 of the UCF warships were at battle stations in Willoughby Bay and Hampton Roads when the naval station was attacked by the ISSA air strike group. For his actions, Devon was later promoted to the rank of Commander and awarded the UCF Navy Commendation Medal.

As ISSA forces began pushing east through Norfolk, ISSA Air Command launched its air strike against Norfolk Naval Station. 66 F-35 Lightning II stealth multi-role fighters, 82 F/A-18E-F Super Hornet twin-engine multirole fighters, and 46 Predator-B/ER unmanned aerial vehicle UAVs were launched from Joint Base McGuire-Dix-Lakehurst air base in New Jersey. The strike group was joined by 3 MQ-4C Triton surveillance UAVs launched from a forward airfield in Delaware.

Expecting to surprise the naval station, the ISSA air strike group instead found the bulk of the UCF fleet at battle stations in Hampton Roads and nearby Willoughby Bay, with RDEW radar-directed energy weapons charged, Phalanx systems active, and its two carriers already deploying fighters.

A fierce aerial battle ensued, concentrated around the carriers, the UCFS Gerald R. Ford and the UCFS John F. Kennedy. Unable to strategically maneuver in the confined waters, the UCF warships had assumed defensive positions around the carriers.

Ford had already launched her entire complement of 64 F-18E/F Super Hornet strike fighters, but the Kennedy was still launching her fighters when the ISSA air strike began. The Kennedy managed to launch only 26 of her fighters before an MK-84 BSU 50 Ballute bomb dropped from an ISSA F-35 struck the ship's port aircraft elevator, crippling the ship.

19 UCAF F-35 Lightning IIs from the nearby Norfolk Naval Air Station joined the battle before ISSA aircraft began engaging the air station. Incredibly, an additional 24 F-35s managed to launch from the air base while under enemy fire.

Within 30 minutes, the UCF situation had become

desperate. Despite having been alerted, more than 20 UCF warships in Hampton Roads and Willoughby Bay had been hit and were on fire, obscuring the bay in thick smoke and hindering the RDEW-equipped cruisers.

Figure 3 - UCAF F-22 Raptor tactical fighter going supersonic above Willoughby Bay during the Battle of Norfolk, April 11, 2041. Image courtesy Norfolk Naval Station Archive.

The Kennedy was listing heavily to port and unable to maneuver. The destroyer James E Williams was on fire and the amphibious assault ship Arlington had been sunk. The destroyer Bainbridge had capsized, and the destroyer Truxtun was going down by the stern.

In the skies above, almost all of the UCAF air cover had been destroyed, and ISSA ground forces were overrunning

Norfolk Naval Station.

At that moment, 58 F-22 Raptor stealth tactical fighters from the UCAF 192nd Fighter Wing unexpectedly arrived from Joint Base Langley-Eustis. The fighters were supported by 31 MQ-9 Reaper UAVs attached to the UCAF 633rd Air Base Wing.

The unexpected UCAF aerial reinforcements swiftly reversed the strategic situation at Norfolk. Surviving ISSA aircraft began to retreat northeast across Chesapeake Bay, while ISSA ground forces in Norfolk halted their advance in confusion.

UCFS Leyte Gulf and Cpt Mark Cory

When the UCAF F-22s reinforcements arrived, Cpt Mark Cory, commanding an aging guided-missile cruiser, the UCFS Leyte Gulf, seized an opportunity to trap the ISSA forces at Norfolk.

Proceeding swiftly east across Hampton Roads, the nearly 50-year old Ticonderoga class cruiser fired 14 of her JMEWS Tomahawk missiles at the dual decks of the Hampton Roads Bridge.

After cutting the bridge to Hampton, Cory directed his ship into Chesapeake Bay and then east, proceeding swiftly towards North Thimble Island.

Retreating ISSA air units, grasping Cory's intentions, now desperately engaged the lone ship. Hit by multiple anti-ship missiles, and with fires raging out of control, the Leyte Gulf managed to fire 11 of her JMEWS Tomahawks at the pylons supporting the Chesapeake Bay Bridge before the ship's launchers were destroyed.

As ISSA aircraft continued to strike the burning ship, Cpt Cory, now severely injured, ordered his crew to continue firing at the bridge decks. "Hammer it, boys! Hammer it!" Cory ordered, before succumbing to his wounds.

Figure 4 - UCF warships in Hampton Roads at the Battle of Norfolk, April 11, 2041. From left to right, the guided-missile cruiser UCFS Leyte Gulf, the guided-missile cruiser UCFS Vella Gulf, and the guided-missile destroyer UCFS James E. Williams (on fire). Two ISSA F/A-18E-F Super Hornets can be seen in the background. This is the last known photograph of the Leyte Gulf. Image courtesy Norfolk Naval Station Archive.

The crew continued their attack, directing fire from an undamaged M242 auto-cannon and the 127mm deck gun at the collapsing bridge, even as the ship began to sink.

14 of the Leyte Gulf's crew were later rescued from the bay, protecting Cory's body in the water.

For his actions, Cpt Cory was posthumously awarded the Navy Cross, and his last command, "Hammer it, boys!" was later adopted as the official base slogan for Norfolk Naval

Station.

Defeat of ISSA Atlantic Command

ISSA Atlantic Command ground forces, now trapped at Norfolk, entrenched themselves at the naval base and in the nearby city.

UCF heavy armor and ground forces attached to Ft. Bragg ComHQ and Ft. Benning ComHQ moved swiftly north to cut the bridges to Portsmouth and Chesapeake, before deploying eastward towards Virginia Beach, effectively trapping the ISSA forces.

While UCAF aircraft harassed the ISSA units in Norfolk day and night, the surviving UCF naval ships blockaded the city to the north and west, preventing any rescue or escape.

After 6 days of intense fighting, the commander of the ISSA Atlantic Command forces in Norfolk surrendered his command.

Casualties and Assessment

The Battle of Norfolk was the largest battle fought in the eastern theater of operations. The battle effectively destroyed the ISSA Atlantic Command, leaving only the ISSA Eastern Command in the region, supported by a significantly reduced ISSA Air Command in the east.

Though eclipsed by later battles in the west, the losses on both sides were not insignificant.

ISSA ground forces sustained 32,441 killed, and 127,502 wounded or captured. More than 1,400 pieces of light armor and 650 pieces of artillery were destroyed or captured, and the ISSA Air Command in the east was devastated, losing more than 160 aircraft.

UCF forces sustained 23,408 killed, nearly half in defense of Norfolk Naval Base itself, and 114,244 wounded. The UCAF lost 116 aircraft, most in defense of the fleet in Hampton Roads and Willoughby Bay. UCF naval units suffered 24 ships sunk or destroyed, including the carrier John F. Kennedy, 4 destroyers, 3 cruisers including the Leyte Gulf, 6 amphibious assault ships, 8 guided-missile destroyers, and 3 sealift command ships.

22 UCF hovercraft were also damaged or destroyed in the initial assault on the Joint Expeditionary Base – Little Creek, though 8 were later repaired and redeployed.

Eastern Campaign

Following its disastrous defeat at the Battle of Norfolk, ISSA Eastern Command's heavy armor units retreated from their positions in northern Pennsylvania and took up defensive positions west of New York City.

Figure 5 - Members of UCF 327th Infantry Regiment assault ISSA Eastern Command forces barricaded inside the Virginia Hospital Center in Arlington, Virginia on August 2, 2041. Image courtesy Scherer American Conflict Museum, Pittsburgh PA, NAFS. File Number 0847K.

UCF Carlisle Armor Groups 4 and 5, and UCF Ft. Bragg Armor Group 3, supported by more than 184,000 troops and 2,600 light armor units gathered from Florida, Georgia, Tennessee, South Carolina, Ohio, and North Carolina, began assembling at Shenandoah National Park in Virginia.

Beginning in early June 2041, with air cover provided by UCAF air units from Joint Base Langley-Eustis in Virginia, and Wright-Patterson Air Force Base in Dayton Ohio, the UCF forces began moving northeast towards Washington D.C.

Figure 6 - UCF soldier's remains within the ashes of the former U.S. Capitol building, September 3, 2041. Image courtesy NAFS American Conflict War Crimes Tribunal Archives. Evidence File 302E4.

In August 2041, with UCF units approaching the city, ISSA Central Committee Attaché Cassandra Cortez and Eastern Regional ISSA Commander Marco Isaacson prepared to abandon the capital.

On August 10, 2041, Cortez and Isaacson instructed the nearby Joint Base Andrews Prison Commandant to remove 474 captured UCF officers from the camp. ISSA forces then set fire to the capitol building before retreating north to Baltimore.

On September 1, 2041, UCF forces liberated the Joint Base Andrews UCF Prison. Of the original 8,233 prisoners, less than half were still alive. The prisoners, malnourished, sick, and suffering from exposure, reported the seizure of their officers the previous month. When UCF forces later searched the burned capitol building, burned bones, charred uniforms, and scorched service tags belonging to the missing officers were found amid the ashes of the former House Chambers.

Over the next three months, combat engagements in the east were limited to skirmishing actions, as ISSA commanders in the region were reluctant to commit their remaining aircraft, armor, or ground forces against the numerically superior UCF units.

By early October 2041, ISSA's eastern leadership had abandoned Baltimore and fled to New York City. UCF forces quickly defeated the remaining ISSA militia units in Maryland and occupied all of Maryland and Delaware south of Delaware Bay.

Battle of Harrisburg

The last significant battle in the eastern region took place on October 9, 2041, at Harrisburg, Pennsylvania.

ISSA heavy armor units, deploying south from New York City, dug in on the east banks of the Susquehanna River in Harrisburg and cut the bridges.

ISSA Eastern Command forces, numbering approximately 62,000 troops, were supported by at least 700 pieces of light armor.

More than 1,900 pieces of field artillery, representing the bulk of ISSA's field artillery units in the east, were deployed in rear positions paralleling the Susquehanna in support of the heavy armor. The artillery pieces consisted primarily of M142 HIMARS rocket launchers, M109A6 155mm Paladin self-propelled howitzers, and M1129 mortar-carrier Strykers.

Figure 7 - ISSA heavy tank on fire near Harrisburg, Pennsylvania, October 11, 2041. Image courtesy Scherer American Conflict Museum, Pittsburgh PA, NAFS. File Number 3301G.

When the UCF heavy armor units arrived, they were met with thunderous fire from the east shore of the Susquehanna River. The UCF units returned file, and a deafening exchange lasting more than 50 hours commenced. UCAF aircraft began engaging the entrenched ISSA tanks and artillery positions. In response, ISSA Air Command committed the last of its eastern aircraft to the battle.

After 3 days, with its armor silenced and its air units destroyed, ISSA forces began retreating from the now-devastated Harrisburg towards New York City.

Defeat of ISSA Eastern Command

As the ISSA ground forces fled north through New York, ISSA Central Committee Attaché Cassandra Cortez and Eastern Regional ISSA Commander Marco Isaacson took sanctuary in the former United Nations building and appealed to the Venezuelan and Ecuadoran governments for asylum.

When their requests were denied, ISSA Naval Command attempted to rescue the trapped ISSA leaders and the city's remaining garrison, but the warships were attacked and destroyed by UCAF aircraft while attempting to maneuver inside the narrow channel at Upper Bay. Cortez and Isaacson were later captured by UCF ground forces hiding inside a closet at the UN building.

Throughout the winter of 2041, UCF ground and air units pursued the remaining ISSA forces north into Quebec, Canada. The Canadian government demanded both sides remove their armed forces from its country, but took no other action, preferring not to antagonize either side in the conflict.

On January 6, 2042, the last ISSA forces in the east surrendered to pursuing UCF units near the tiny town of Dryden, in western Ontario, Canada.

Casualties and Assessment

The Eastern Campaign, as it was later called, resulted in the destruction or capture of all ISSA forces in the eastern region.

During the campaign, ISSA sustained 84,503 troops killed, with an additional 192,240 troops captured or wounded (including regional militia and state guard units).

More than 105 heavy tanks, 1,205 pieces of light armor, and 2,200 pieces of field artillery were destroyed or captured.

ISSA Air Command lost more than 115 aircraft in combat, with an additional 72 aircraft captured on the ground.

ISSA Naval Command lost 16 ships during the eastern campaign, most at Upper Bay in New York City while attempting to evacuate ISSA leadership and the city garrison. Losses included 5 guided-missile frigates, 4 destroyers, 1 cruiser, 3 amphibious assault ships, and 3 sealift command ships.

UCF casualties during the eastern campaign were 68,520 troops killed, and 133,404 wounded. Equipment losses were 62 heavy tanks, 1,151 pieces of light armor, and 628 pieces of field artillery.

USAF Command lost 96 aircraft in combat, most over Harrisburg Pennsylvania.

The UCF lost no naval ships to combat action during the Eastern Campaign, but it did lose an Arleigh Burke-class guided-missile destroyer, the UCFS Gravely, when one of its MH-60S helicopters crashed against the ship's superstructure in high winds, igniting fires that spread to the ship's Mark 41 VLS silos, detonating several missiles.

Siege of Boise

On April 8, 2041, ISSA North-Western Command began moving light armor and ground forces southeast through Washington state and Oregon to staging areas in the Rye Valley in eastern Oregon.

At the same time, ISSA Air Command began assembling aircraft at Kingsley Field Air Force Base near Klamath Falls, Oregon.

<u>Raid on Mountain Home Air Force Base</u>

On the evening of April 10, ISSA North-Western Command launched 40 Defiant and 38 older V-22 Osprey transport helicopters from Rome Airfield in southwestern Oregon.

The force, carrying a mixed contingent of approximately 950 commandos and 100 construction engineers was supported by a dozen S-97 Raiders. Flying low to avoid UCF radar, the force was landed approximately 4 km west of then UCF-held Mountain Home Air Force Base in southwestern Idaho.

Following the outbreak of hostilities in March, 14 F-35s attached to the former USA 366th Fighter Wing at Mountain Home AFB had defected to join ISSA Air Command units in the west. The remaining 44 F-35s at the base were subsequently relocated to Hill Air Force Base in Utah to join the UCAF aircraft assembling there.

In order to prevent ISSA Air Command from using the now abandoned Mountain Home AFB, its airstrip was ordered bulldozed and rendered unusable for fixed-wing flight operations.

In the pre-dawn hours of April 11, the ISSA commandos attacked the base. The depleted garrison, consisting of only 600 lightly-armed militia units attached to the UCF-Idaho National Guard, and assorted civilian contractors tasked with the airfield's destruction, were quickly overwhelmed.

Figure 8 - Remains of UCF-Idaho National Guardsmen and civilian contractors massacred at Mountain Home Air Force Base on April 11, 2041. Image courtesy NAFS American Conflict War Crimes Tribunal Archives. Evidence File 303E19.

In one of the first incidents of ISSA war crimes committed during the Conflict, the ISSA commandos forced the surviving UCF and civilian personnel into one of the field hangers. Then, as Chinook C-47F helicopters began to arrive with M9 Earthmovers and other equipment for the ISSA construction crews, the commandos began firing through the hanger's corrugated tin walls and windows at the men inside. Later, the ISSA construction engineers drove their M9s through the hanger, destroying the building and crushing those still alive under the equipment's heavy tracks.

Siege of Boise

With the base secured, the construction engineers began repairing the airfield. At that same time, ISSA North-Western Command forces began moving east from their staging areas in the Rye Valley towards Boise Idaho.

Pushing swiftly through Caldwell and Nampa Idaho, ISSA reconnaissance units had reached the outskirts of Boise Idaho by mid-morning. Anticipating little to no resistance, the units began advancing into the city but were immediately engaged by elements of the UCF-Idaho National Guard.

The 4,000 lightly-armed guardsmen, under the command of Cpt Bob Ford, had hastily mobilized following a report of ISSA units assembling in western Oregon. The guardsmen fought furiously, destroying 4 MPF mobile protected firepower light tanks, and 3 RCV remote combat vehicles.

Believing they were engaging regular UCF ground forces, the advancing ISSA reconnaissance units withdrew west of Meridian Road to wait for reinforcements.

During the brief delay, Ford opened the national guard armories to the city leaders and called for the formation of a local militia under Boise City Councilman Marcus Phelps. Within 24 hours, more than 32,000 militia members had been armed and deployed to key strategic positions within the city.

Without heavy armor to confront the entrenched defenders, ISSA commanders deployed their artillery units, consisting of 74 M142 HIMARS rocket launchers, 80 M109A6 155mm Paladins, 33 DSLP drone-swarming launch platforms, and 98 M1129 Mortar Carrier Strykers, supported by nearly 60 S-97 Raider and older AH-1Z attack helicopters.

The city defenders returned fire with an assortment of aging M252 mortars, FIM-92E Stinger missiles, M40 105mm recoilless rifles, a handful of MPF mobile protected firepower light tanks, and approximately 180 pieces of antiquated artillery pieces hastily placed back into service following the outbreak of hostilities the previous month. With no DTAG drone-targeting auto-gun "swatters", the city defenders were forced to rely on 2-man tc-shot teams to counter the ISSA drones.

Figure 9 - UCF militiamen aid a friend during the Siege of Boise, April 16, 2041. Image courtesy Scherer American Conflict Museum, Pittsburgh PA, NAFS. File Number 7782P.

For 8 days, the Boise defenders desperately engaged the heavily-armed ISSA forces. Battles raged street to street, house to house. Finally, on March 19, the remaining guardsmen and militia, barricaded inside their command post at the old Boise State University stadium building, exhausted and out of ammunition, surrendered. Cpt Ford radioed the surrender himself, and, helping the wounded Phelps, the two men escorted the surviving defenders from the building under a white flag.

Word had arrived 2 days earlier of the ISSA Atlantic Command's catastrophic defeat and surrender at Norfolk Virginia. When ISSA North-Western Commandant Evan McConnell discovered the city defenders were merely regional guardsmen and militia, frustrated and outraged, he pulled his pistol and executed Ford. When Phelps protested, McConnell executed him also.

Chaos erupted, as ISSA troops, emboldened by their Commandant's actions, began shooting the surrendered defenders. Urged on by Central Committee Attaché Katherine Wyden's shouts to "take no prisoners!", the ISSA forces surged through the now-defenseless city.

For nearly 30 hours, the city's residents were subjected to an orgy of rape, murder, fire, and looting by the unrestrained ISSA forces. Tens of thousands of residents were killed. Thousands more fled into the foothills to the northeast, where they listened to the screams rising from their burning city.

For her part in encouraging the massacre, ISSA Central Committee Attaché Wyden was later convicted of war crimes at the Provisional NAFS War Crimes Tribunal in Ft. Benning and hanged. ISSA Commandant McConnell, though he did not survive the Conflict, was also posthumously convicted of war crimes.

In honor of the sacrifices made by national guard and local

militia forces during the conflict, a statue of Cpt Ford, assisting a wounded Councilman Phelps, was later raised at the American Conflict Memorial in Washington D.C.

Casualties and Assessment

ISSA casualties at what later became known as the Siege of Boise were 18,244 killed, 32,008 wounded. ISSA lost 3 M142 HIMARS rocket launchers, 8 DSLP drone swarm launch platforms, 5 M109A6 155mm Paladin self-propelled howitzers, 7 MPF mobile protected firepower light tanks, 8 RCV remote combat vehicles, 1 SHORAD short-range air defense Stryker, and 9 assorted APC armored personnel carriers.

The UCF-Idaho National Guard garrison at Boise was almost entirely destroyed. Only 16 of the 4,000 guardsmen survived the battle, hidden by brave local residents. Local militia casualties could not be accurately counted but were estimated to be at least 32,000 killed.

At least 78,000 civilians were killed, with as many as 40,000 of the deaths occurring after the city fell to ISSA forces.

Battle of Utah

While the ISSA North-Western Command forces were engaged at nearby Boise, ISSA construction engineers at Mountain Home Air Force Base were busy repairing its airfield. After 3 days, with the airfield now operational, the first of the ISSA Air Command aircraft began to arrive from Kingsley Field Air Force Base in Klamath Falls, Oregon.

On April 21, ISSA North-Western Command forces in Boise began reassembling southeast of the burning city. They were joined by transport units from Portland, Oregon bringing munitions, fuel, and nearly 110,000 reinforcements.

On April 26, ISSA North-Western Command, now numbering more than 185,000 ground units, and supported by more than 1,400 pieces of light armor, began moving east. The force crossed the Snake River at the (evacuated) city of Twin Falls Idaho and then turned south onto the State Route 93 towards Nevada.

Initially, UCF commanders in the region were uncertain as to ISSA's objectives. It was speculated that the force might be moving south to link up with the massive ISSA forces coming out of Southern California. Communities as far south as Las Vegas Nevada were warned to prepare to evacuate.

When the force turned east at Wells, Nevada, however, UCF Dugway ComHQ issued an invasion alert for the state of Utah, mobilizing all UCF, guard, and militia forces in the "Deseret" region.

Battle of Utah

After the capture of Mountain Home AFB on April 11, UCF Dugway ComHQ deployed forward observation units to strategic locations in southern Idaho, northern Utah, and northern Nevada, to monitor ISSA movements.

Figure 10 - Fighter craft above the Wasatch Mountain range during the Battle of Utah, April 30, 2041. Image courtesy Scherer American Conflict Museum, Pittsburgh PA, NAFS. File Number 1104D.

One unit, parachuted into the Snake River Valley near Hammett Idaho, had moved west along the river and established an observation post at the northern-most curve of the river above CJ Strike Reservoir, approximately 3 kilometers southwest of Mountain Home AFB. From there, the unit had deployed its ROMD remote operated micro-drone "bugs" into the base.

On the morning of April 30, the UCF "buggers" observed

nearly 300 ISSA aircraft at the base being readied for launch and transmitted the information to UCF Dugway ComHQ. At 04:30, the aircraft began launching from the base.

Hoping to draw UCAF fighter aircraft from Hill Air Force Base into the range of its SHORAD short-range air defense Strykers approaching from the west, ISSA Air Command launched a group of Predator-B/ER UAVs southeast at an altitude of 2,000 meters directly towards UCF Dugway ComHQ.

The remaining ISSA air strike group flew low to the southeast. The group intended to approach Hill AFB covertly, using the Wasatch Mountain Range for cover, and then emerge from the mouth of nearby Weber Canyon to surprise the unsuspecting base.

Minutes after launching its air strike group, however, ISSA's observation units, operating from a concealed location near Weber Canyon, reported UCAF fighter aircraft launching en masse from Hill AFB, heading north over the Wasatch Mountains.

Realizing its attack had been discovered, ISSA Air Command ordered its strike aircraft to engage the UCF aircraft. It redirected its Predator UAV group eastward and launched 180 older F/A-18 Hornets from Edwards Air Force Base in southern California. It then readied a secondary air strike group; 4 B-21 Raider long-range strike bombers at Beale Air Force Base.

What followed was the largest air battle of the American Conflict. For almost five hours, nearly 800 combat aircraft battled for supremacy in the skies above northern Utah. As fighter aircraft chased each other through the narrow, twisting canyons of the Wasatch mountains, F/A-18 Hornets from ISSA's Edwards AFB strike group concentrated their attack on Hill Air Force Base itself.

After nearly 5 hours, the base's RDEW radar-directed energy weapons and its Raytheon LAD laser air defenses had been destroyed, and its SDDN swarm-drone defense net was almost completely depleted.

As UCAF units on the ground scrambled to deploy reserve SHORAD short-range air defense Strykers, the ISSA B-21s from Beale AFB approached from the west.

Nuclear Strike

UCAF Lt Co Gary "Rowdy" Smith, commanding UCAF 4th Fighter Squadron at Hill AFB, had just ducked his F-35 Lightning II fighter into Weber Canyon with two ISSA F-22 Raptors in pursuit when a B-61 Mod 12 tactical nuclear bomb struck the base.

Stunned, burned, and disoriented from the concussion, Smith struggled to pull his damaged aircraft out of the canyon. Expecting to be shot down at any moment by the pursuing Raptors, Smith instead found himself alone, as both of the chasing aircraft had been downed by the estimated 100kt blast.

Calling for 4th Squadron to immediately re-form and pursue the B-21s, Smith engaged his F-35's after-burner. As he closed on the ISSA bombers, now turning towards Salt Lake City, the two sole surviving members of UCAF 4th Fighter Squadron, Lt. Jake "Dusty" Martin, and Capt. Richard "Speedy" Gonzales raced to follow.

Closing range on the bombers, Smith attempted to fire an AIM-9X Sidewinder missile at the trailing B-21 but discovered his aircraft's fire control system had been damaged by the blast. After ordering the following wingmen to "bring the bastards down!", Smith deliberately dove his F-35 into the aft-superstructure of the rearmost B-21, destroying the bomber.

Smith's trailing wingmen, themselves pursued by ISSA aircraft, managed to bring down the remaining three B-21s, two with AIM-9X missile strikes, and the last by Gonzales with multiple hits from his F-35's GAU-22A cannon.

Both Martin and Gonzales survived the battle to tell the story of Lt Col Smith's sacrifice (*See: "The Fighting Fuujins Over Utah" – by J. C. Alton; NAFS-Archive Unit 72, 24m - (ar) 2104, File: 7E0AC7FA5*).

After the nuclear strike on Hill Air Force Base, UCAF commanders realized they were facing an entirely new war. All surviving UCAF aircraft were immediately ordered to disengage and attempt to reach Schriever or Buckley air base in Colorado.

Those too low on fuel or otherwise unable to reach Colorado were ordered to attempt to reach civilian airfields in Wyoming or eastern Idaho.

The Mormon Militia

Throughout the early days of the American Conflict, the Mormon Church in Utah, constituting nearly 58% of the state's entire population at that time, had struggled to maintain the church's neutrality in the conflict.

When word reached church leaders of the ISSA atrocities in Boise, however, the church capitulated. Describing ISSA as the "greatest evil of our day", church leaders authorized the immediate formation of two separate member militia units; the "Army of Deseret", and the "Mormon Battalion".

Though created under the authority of the church's leadership, military control of both militia units was released to UCF Dugway ComHQ. The Army of Deseret, numbering approximately 45,000 older militia members, would garrison

Salt Lake City and the surrounding cities, while the Mormon Battalion, numbering almost 110,000 members, would be sent southwest to reinforce the 65,000 UCF and national guard units already at Dugway.

When UCF Dugway ComHQ issued its invasion alert for the State of Utah, both militia units were swiftly mobilized. The following day, as the aerial battle played out in the skies above, the Mormon Battalion militia was already on state transway 199 moving swiftly towards Dugway.

Capture of Dugway ComHQ

Moving south along state transway 196, ISSA North-Western Command forces reached the Dugway Proving Grounds in the early morning hours of May 1.

Expecting to find only 65,000 UCF and national guard troops supported by a few hundred pieces of light armor, ISSA commanders found themselves facing a ground force nearly as numerically large as their own, though considerably less well-equipped.

As the UCF and militia units scrambled to entrench themselves, ISSA armored units engaged the base.

The battle for Dugway was bloody, fierce, and short. Though the base defenders fought heroically, they were no match for ISSA's numerically superior and better-equipped force.

By 11:00, with his forward companies already falling back, UCF Dugway ComHQ Base Commander Hendricks ordered all UCF, guardsmen, and militia forces to retreat eastward and join regional garrisons assembling in Orem and Provo. Hendricks also ordered the destruction of all of the base's chemical and biological weapon research and lab facilities.

Though aware of the fate of the captured militiamen in Boise, six hundred of the Mormon Battalion militia members volunteered to remain behind to cover the UCF retreat and complete the research facility's destruction.

When ISSA forces finally entered the base at 14:20, ISSA Commandant Evan McConnell ordered his forces not to pursue the retreating UCF and militia units, but to secure the base and its research facilities. When he discovered the facilities had been destroyed, McConnell ordered his forces to tie the 83 surviving militiamen to posts along transway 199 and personally executed the men.

Casualties and Assessment

With UCF Hill Air Force Base destroyed, and UCF Dugway ComHQ now under ISSA control, the Battle of Utah came to an end. The battle was a significant victory for ISSA Central Command, who used the engagement to reassure its military and civilian population after the demoralizing defeat at the Battle of Norfolk.

While it succeeded in achieving its military and political objectives, ISSA failed to achieve its secondary (clandestine) objective of capturing the chemical and biological weapons research and development facilities at Dugway.

ISSA losses during the Battle of Utah were 24,288 ground forces killed, 47,702 wounded, and 933 captured or missing. Approximately 80 pieces of light armor were also destroyed.

ISSA Air Command lost 4 B-21 strategic bombers and 294 miscellaneous combat aircraft in the skies over Utah.

UCF and guardsmen losses were 18,332 ground forces and national guardsmen killed, most in defense of Dugway ComHQ. Of the 33,501 wounded during the battle, almost all made it to Orem or Provo.

Mormon Battalion militia losses were 26,494 killed at Dugway, including the 600 volunteers who covered the UCF retreat. 31,211 militia were wounded, but like the UCF and guardsmen wounded, most survived to reached Orem or Provo.

The UCAF lost 259 aircraft to combat action during the battle, including 14 aircraft on the ground when Hill AFB was destroyed. 46 UCAF aircraft reached safe airfields in the east.

More than 19,300 aircrew, service personnel, security, and civilian contractors were killed in the tactical nuclear strike on Hill Air Force Base. More than 48,000 civilians in the surrounding communities were also killed in the blast, with an additional 102,000 injured.

International Reaction to the Nuclear Strike

International reaction to ISSA's nuclear strike on UCAF Hill Air Force Base was swift but largely impotent.

Under the terms of the International Agreement of the American Combatants (IAAC), both ISSA and the Ft. Bragg Congress had explicitly disclaimed the use of chemical, biological, and nuclear weapons during the conflict.

Under pressure from the world's nuclear-armed nations, both sides had surrendered operational, though not physical control, of all USA intercontinental ballistic nuclear missiles to a hastily-constituted custodial body, the International Nuclear Force Commission (INFC), consisting of 5 former United Nation members friendly to the USA (Great Britain, France, Japan, Germany, and Canada). All USA missile launch codes were re-coded and secured with the INFC.

While the INFC held operational control of all land and sea-borne inter-continental ballistic missiles, the country's arsenal of nuclear gravity bombs remained uncontrolled and in the hands of the combatants.

Following the nuclear strike on Hill AFB, the INFC declared ISSA to be in breach of the Ottawa agreement and immediately ordered the ISSA Central Committee to surrender all nuclear weapons under its control.

The demand was ignored.

Sonoran Offensive

In the early morning hours of April 25, UCF ROMD remote operated micro-drone bugs in the small town of Indio, California transmitted images of massive ISSA forces moving east on Interstate 10 towards Arizona. For almost 8 hours, the bug operators recorded more than 340 heavy tanks, 4,250 pieces of light armor, and an estimated 480,000 ground forces moving through the small town.

Three days later, on April 28, bug operators near the northern border town of Needles, California reported a second ISSA force crossing east into northern Arizona on Interstate 40. That "northern" force consisted of more than 150 heavy tanks, 2,500 pieces of light armor, and an estimated 200,000 troops.

UCF Houston ComHQ responded by issuing an invasion alert for Arizona and New Mexico. The 90,370 UCF ground forces stationed in Phoenix were put on alert, and the nearly 190,000 guardsmen and local militia units began deploying to key city support positions.

At 05:30 on May 3, UCF reconnaissance units in the desert west of Phoenix spotted advance ISSA forces approaching the valley and communicated the information to UCF Houston ComHQ. Multiple UCAF air bases were placed on alert, including Yuma Air Station, Luke Air Force Base west of Phoenix, and Davis-Monthan Air Force Base in Tucson.

Nuclear Strikes on Phoenix

At approximately 05:42, as UCAF F-35 Lightning IIs were preparing to launch from Luke Air Force Base, a squadron of ISSA F-22 Raptors was observed closing swiftly from the west.

The Raptors, flying low with their afterburners engaged,

had just cleared the White Tank Mountains and were racing towards central Phoenix when a B-83 nuclear bomb dropped from one of the Raptors struck the base.

Figure 11 - ISSA nuclear strike on UCAF Luke Air Force Base, western Phoenix Arizona, May 3, 2041. Photo taken from nearby Estrella Mtn by Sgt Gerald Beal, UCF 75th Rangers. Image courtesy Scherer American Conflict Museum, Pittsburgh PA, NAFS. File Number 0223H.

The 1.2Mt blast was heard as far away as Tucson and created a fireball more than a kilometer in diameter. The surrounding cities of El Mirage, Sun City, Peoria, Goodyear, Waddell, Avondale, and Litchfield Park were devastated.

The warhead, detonating approximately 300m above the

base, killed more than 108,000 people and injured more than 306,000 others. At least 90 combat aircraft at Luke Air Force Base were destroyed, and more than 22,000 base personnel and their family members were killed.

A few seconds later, a second B-83 bomb dropped from the Raptors detonated above Phoenix Sky Harbor International Airport.

This second blast destroyed buildings as far east as Gilbert and Chandler and killed more than 321,000 people. An additional 738,000 were injured in the explosion.

As Phoenix was being devastated by the dual nuclear strikes, an ISSA air strike group flying out of Beale Air Force Base in southern California attacked the UCAF Air Station in Yuma, destroying more than 80 UCAF aircraft in aerial combat before ISSA forces on the ground captured the base.

By afternoon, with fires raging out of control throughout the city of Phoenix, a massive ISSA force closing from the west, and the Salt River basin filling with burned victims seeking relief from their injuries, the "Valley of the Sun" began to self-evacuate.

Operation "Desert Tortoise"

When word reached the Ft. Bragg Congressional leaders of the nuclear strikes in Utah and Arizona, despite calls for restraint from the international community, it granted nuclear release-authority to regional UCF commanders.

The ISSA forces approaching Phoenix ultimately circumvented the valley, moving south along Phoenix Bypass Route 85 to Interstate 10. As the ISSA force moved southeast towards Tucson, Davis-Monthan Air Force Base, the last UCAF combat air group in Arizona, began preparing for an assault.

At 10:30 on May 10, ISSA F-22s and F-35s flying from the captured Yuma Air Station were detected approaching Davis-Monthan Air Force Base. The base's venerable 12th Air Force Group launched its fighter aircraft and engaged the ISSA aircraft approximately 160km west of the base.

Thought the UCAF pilots fought valiantly, their older F/A-18 Hornets were no match for the more-advanced and numerically superior ISSA F-22 Raptors and F-35 Lightning IIs. Within thirty minutes, more than half of the UCAF aircraft had been destroyed, and ground personnel at the base began activating the base's RDEW radar-directed energy weapons, Raytheon LAD laser air defenses, and SDDN swarming-drone defensive net in preparation for a strike against the base itself.

As the aerial battle played out west of the base, Col Andrew "Snoopy" Schultz (retired), and four other reserve UCAF pilots initiated "Operation Desert Tortoise".

Flying archaic A-10C "Warthogs", the five grey-haired pilots flew to the southeast, keeping low to the desert floor. Gaining altitude swiftly as they approached Davidson Canyon, Col Shultz dropped a B-61 Mod-12 GPS-guided earth-penetrating nuclear bomb at the canyon floor near the Mescal Arroyo transport bridges.

The reinforced bomb, dropped from an altitude of 2,000 meters, penetrated deeply into the ground before detonating. The resulting 50 kiloton explosion destroyed the roads and bridges inside the canyon, and partially collapsed several of its cliffs, rendering the canyon impassable.

The A-10s pushed east, dropping 9 similar warheads at other transportation choke points, before flying on to land at a remote service airfield in New Mexico.

Within an hour, Davis-Monthan AFB fell to the advancing

ISSA forces, and all surviving UCAF aircraft were ordered to attempt to reach airfields in New Mexico or Texas.

<u>5-Month Halt</u>

Faced with the prospect of moving hundreds of thousands of its ground forces on foot through the extreme southern-Arizona heat, ISSA's Central Committee ordered its Western Command forces to hold at Tucson, Arizona and Albuquerque, New Mexico.

During what became a 5-month halt, international efforts to resolve the conflict increased, but ultimately proved unsuccessful.

On September 20, the ISSA Central Committee leaders in San Francisco delivered an ultimatum, demanding the Ft. Bragg Congress recognize ISSA independence and threatening complete annihilation if its demands were ignored or refused.

The Ft. Bragg Congress's formal response, approved by unanimous vote of the legislature, and transmitted by Joint Capitalist Force Commander, General John Hilbrands, was, "Go fuck yourselves."

<u>Nuclear Strikes on El Paso</u>

On October 8, ISSA Western Command's "southern" force in Tucson, now reinforced to nearly 800,000 ground troops, began moving east across the southern Arizona desert, leaving behind 100,000 troops to garrison Tucson.

By October 28, UCF reconnaissance units reported the force had reached Lordsburg, New Mexico.

On November 2, UCAF reconnaissance aircraft reported that the "northern" force, moving south from Albuquerque,

New Mexico, had reached the town of Cuchillo.

UCF Houston ComHQ began moving hundreds of heavy tanks, accompanied by thousands of light armor, artillery, and ground forces from staging areas towards El Paso, Texas,

UCF commanders intended to engage the advancing ISSA groups near Las Cruces, New Mexico, supported by aircraft launched from nearby Holloman Air Force Base.

At 01:17 on November 3, UCAF patrol aircraft, flying approximately 200 kilometers west of Holloman AFB, detected an intermittent radar signal approaching fast from the west and informed Houston ComHQ.

Anticipating an incoming ISSA air strike, launch orders were immediately transmitted to Holloman AFB, who began launching its fighter aircraft while ground personnel activated the base's anti-air defenses.

Six minutes later, 8 ISSA B-21 bombers, escorted by a squadron of F-22 Raptors, roared over the base, dropping a B-61 Mod-12 tactical nuclear bomb in their wake.

39 of the base's F-22 Raptors had managed to launch before the bomb struck. The detonation lit up the night sky, blinding several of the UCAF pilots who had not secured their TFPD visors. The surviving UCAF Raptors engaged the ISSA air strike group, which had immediately turned south towards El Paso.

As Raptor fought Raptor in the dark skies above, Raytheon LAD laser air defenses, RDEW radar-directed energy weapons, and SHORAD short-range air defense Strykers positioned outside El Paso desperately tried to knock down the approaching bombers.

Three of the eight B-21s survived, each dropping a B-61 Mod 12 nuclear bomb on the city.

McFarlane's Retaliatory Nuclear Strike

Following the triple nuclear detonations at El-Paso, the ISSA aircraft disengaged. The surviving UCAF F-22 Raptors reassembled and began to retreat east towards UCAF Goodfellow Air Force Base. Minutes into their flight, however, they received contravening orders from Houston ComHQ.

In accordance with standing operational orders following ISSA's earlier nuclear strikes in Phoenix, four of the UCAF F-22 Raptors were carrying a B-61 Mod 12 nuclear bomb in their main internal weapons bay. UCF Houston ComHQ immediately ordered the remaining aircraft to attempt a retaliatory nuclear strike on the ISSA Western Command forces approaching from the north.

The F-22 group's senior surviving officer, UCAF Maj Bud "Mongrel" McFarlane, ordered his 14 wingmen to take up protecting positions below the 4 nuclear-armed F-22s as they approached the ISSA forces outside the small town of Garfield.

A UCAF radar tracking station concealed on nearby Timber Mountain recorded McFarlane's wingmen held their protecting formations, even as multiple ISSA anti-aircraft missiles began decimating the approaching aircraft.

At least two of the nuclear-armed F-22s survived long enough to drop their B-61 nuclear bombs on the approaching ISSA force. The following day, UCAF reconnaissance aircraft observed scattered ISSA heavy and light armor units retreating north to Albuquerque.

None of McFarlane's air group survived the attack.

Casualties and Assessment

The nuclear strikes on El Paso killed more than 650,000

civilians and injured more than a million others.

UCF forces in the city were devastated, losing an estimated 203,000 ground units, more than 260 heavy tanks, 1,100 pieces of light armor, and 1,650 artillery pieces.

The destruction of El Paso signaled the end of what later became known as the "Sonoran Offensive". While ISSA Western Command's "northern" group was almost entirely destroyed in Maj McFarlane's retaliatory air strike, it's much larger "southern" group was virtually untouched.

As the massive ISSA force now approached the west Texas border, UCF Houston ComHQ issued an invasion alert for the state of Texas.

Gulf Retreat

With the destruction of its forces at El Paso, Texas, UCF Houston ComHQ was facing a strategic crisis.

UCF commanders had almost no heavy armor units remaining outside of Houston itself. UCF regional light armor forces numbered less than 2,000 assorted MPF mobile-protected firepower light tanks, RCV remote combat vehicles, assorted Strykers, DSLP drone-swarming launch platforms, APC armored personnel carriers, and aging Bradley fighting vehicles. Most were manned by inexperienced guardsmen, and in some cases, local militia units.

UCAF aircraft in the region had been reduced to only 45 F-35s, 34 F-22 Raptors, and a collection of 65 F/A-18 Hornets, F-15 Eagles, and F-16 Falcons, supported by approximately 55 MH-6M Little Bird and S-97 Raider attack helicopters.

The aircraft were disbursed among a handful of air force bases in central Texas, while reserve air units, including aging A-10 "warthogs", UH-60M Blackhawks, and AH-64F Apache helicopters, were assembled in secondary, service, or civilian airfields.

UCF ground forces in San Antonio, including its enthusiastic, though ill-equipped, 68,000-strong "Sam Houston Militia", numbered only 123,000 troops.

Dallas/Ft. Worth had 165,000 assorted UCF, national guard, and militia units.

UCF ground units in Houston, though better-armed, totaled a mere 86,000 troops.

Austin was garrisoned entirely by 34,000 guardsmen and local militia.

By December 2, ISSA Western Command forces had reached

Sheffield Texas, approximately 400 kilometers from San Antonio.

Mexico's Entry into the American Conflict

On December 9, 2041, UCAF patrol aircraft flying from Laughlin AFB near the Rio Grande river, reported large numbers of Mexican troops assembling near the border town of La Potasa, Coahuila in Mexico.

UCAF Reconnaissance aircraft sent to investigate reported an estimated 110,000 Mexican troops already in the town, supported by at least 950 pieces of light armor.

Additional concentrations of Mexican troops were later discovered assembling near Ojinaga, Chihuahua, and Nuevo Laredo, Tamaulipas.

Congressional leaders at the Ft. Bragg Congress demanded an explanation for the troop movements from the Mexican government but received no reply.

At 04:30 on December 16, 2041, ISSA Western Command forces began moving from their staging areas near Sheffield. At the same time, UCAF reconnaissance aircraft reported advance units of Mexican forces from La Potasa, Coahuila and Nuevo Laredo, Tamaulipas, crossing the Rio Grande river into Texas.

At 05:00 that morning, the Mexican ambassador to the Ft. Bragg Congress delivered the Mexican government's "Declaración de San Jacinto", announcing Mexico's recognition of ISSA sovereignty, and its mutual defense agreement with ISSA armed forces.

The Gulf Retreat

UCF Houston ComHQ immediately ordered all UCF,

national guard, and militia forces in western Texas to retreat south to Corpus Christi. UCAF aircraft were ordered to cover the retreat and then assemble at the Houston International Airport. At the same time, UCF forces in Houston began preparing to retreat south to Galveston.

During what later became known as the "Gulf Retreat", UCAF aircraft made three separate attempts to strike ISSA Western Command forces with nuclear warheads, however, their air strike groups were annihilated by SHORAD short-range air defense equipped Strykers, THAAD terminal high-altitude air defense units, and the numerically-superior ISSA air units.

After losing virtually all of its remaining F-22 Raptors in the three failed nuclear strikes, UCF Houston ComHQ issued orders for all UCF forces in the region to commence "delaying actions". At the same time, UCF naval units raced south from Norfolk to try and reach evacuation ports in Corpus Christi and Galveston via the Gulf of Mexico.

UCF special service units began placing nuclear mines ahead of the approaching ISSA forces at key strategic crossroads throughout central Texas. Several mines successfully detonated, destroying auxiliary ISSA units near El Dorado, Rocksprings, and Brady Texas, but the main ISSA force continued towards Houston.

The Sam Houston Militia in San Antonio refused to abandon the city. Shouting "Alamo" as they waved farewell to the UCF troops and guardsmen, the 68,000 militiamen entrenched themselves within the city.

On December 22, the Mexican and ISSA forces met approximately 6 kilometers west of San Antonio. By prior agreement of their leaders, ISSA Western Command ordered its units to bypass the city and permit the Mexican forces to subdue the city's defenders. With its Mexican allies engaged at San Antonio, ISSA Western Command forces continued east towards Houston.

On December 26, word reached UCF leaders in Houston of an ISSA nuclear strike on its forces in Corpus Christi. More than 91,000 UCF guardsmen and militia were killed, with at least 52 UCAF aircraft and 464 pieces of light armor destroyed. The blast also killed more than 88,000 civilians and injured more than 194,000 others.

By December 29, nearly a million ISSA Western Command and Mexican forces were assembled near La Grange, Texas, only 160km west of Houston, in preparation for the final assault on the city.

In San Antonio, the besieged militia defenders had retreated to their last defensive positions around their command post inside the San Antonio International Airport.

Anticipating a nuclear strike, Houston's civilian population had evacuated the city.

The Sino-Ft. Bragg Compact

At 06:45 on January 1, 2042, UCF radio operators in Houston received a brief communique from Joint Capitalist Forces Command Headquarters in Ft. Bragg, ordering all UCF commanders to stand by for an important announcement.

At 07:00 Houston local time, the Ft. Bragg Congress announced it had signed a mutual trade and defense compact with the People's Republic of China.

Within the hour, UCF naval units operating in the Pacific reported the first Chinese troop landings on the west coast of California

Sino – Ft. Bragg Compact

The Sino – Ft. Bragg Compact was a mutual trade and defense agreement between the People's Republic of China and the Provisional Ft. Bragg Congress *(See: "The Sino Compact of 2041"; NAFS-Archive Unit 09, 3s - (ar) 2082, Summary File: BBA966B1B2).*

The agreement, signed on December 2, 2041, in Ottawa, Canada, promised immediate Chinese military support to the UCF war effort, in exchange for long-term trade, technical cooperation, and economic concessions favorable to expanding Chinese business and manufacturing interests in the west.

The announcement of the Compact and the resulting landing of Chinese military forces on the west coast had an immediate and dramatic effect on the American Conflict, effectively bringing the war to a swift, though devastating conclusion.

Collapse of ISSA

By January 7, 2042, more than a million Chinese troops had been landed at dozens of debarkation areas along the west coast of California, Oregon, and Washington. By January 15, more than 3 million Chinese troops had landed, accompanied by thousands of pieces of light armor, artillery, and more than 200 combat aircraft.

Figure 12 - People's Republic of China forces landing at Hermosa Beach, California, January 4, 2042. Image courtesy 中华人民共和国 美国冲突博物馆 *(People's Republic of China - American Conflict Museum in Beijing).*

ISSA Western Command forces in Texas immediately began pulling back towards New Mexico, abandoning its planned assault on Houston.

With the hasty departure of the ISSA units, Mexican forces in the region became disheartened and began withdrawing from

San Antonio. UCF Houston ComHQ immediately ordered all regional UCF, national guard, and militia units to pursue and engage the Mexican forces.

Figure 13 - People's Republic of China armored units firing at ISSA positions near Portland, Oregon, February 3, 2042. Image courtesy 中华人民共和国 美国冲突 博物馆 *(People's Republic of China - American Conflict Museum in Beijing).*

By January 11, 2042, the Mexican forces had retreated back across the Rio Grande river, pursued by UCF air and ground units.

With tens of thousands of hostile forces pouring across the border into its northern states, the Mexican government quickly capitulated, sending peace envoys to Ft. Bragg.

ISSA North-Western Command forces in Utah began retreating west through Nevada, leaving a trail of burned towns and civilian atrocities in their wake.

On January 22, while approaching Fernley, Nevada, ISSA's North-Western Command group was intercepted by 8 Chinese Xian H-6K bombers launched hours earlier from the UCAF-aligned Anderson Air Force Base in Guam.

Under the terms of the Sino-Ft. Bragg Compact, China was prohibited from deploying its own nuclear weapons in the conflict, but it was permitted to assist UCF forces with facilitating their own nuclear strikes.

As the Chinese bombers approached Fernley, ISSA commanders hastily activated their THAAD terminal high altitude air defense platforms. UCAF ordnance specialists on the aircraft managed to drop 4 GPS-guided B-83 nuclear bombs on the ISSA forces before the missiles struck. The massive detonations shattered windows as far away as Sacramento.

Five of the attacking Chinese bombers were destroyed during the strike, but the remaining 3 survived to land at UCAF Minot Air Force Base in North Dakota.

The following morning, UCAF reconnaissance aircraft flying over Arizona reported ISSA Western Command had split its remaining force at Casa Grande, Arizona into two separate groups. One group was moving west along Phoenix Bypass Route 8 towards Yuma, Arizona. The second group was moving north towards Phoenix.

At 16:30 that afternoon, the 3 surviving Chinese Xian H-6K bombers, now refueled and re-armed at Minot AFB, and accompanied by 30 F-22 Raptor reinforcements newly arrived from the east, struck the Yuma-bound ISSA group with 3 B-61 Mod 12 nuclear bombs.

Flying on, the strike group dropped a B-61 Mod 11 "low yield" bomb on the ISSA-controlled Yuma Air Station.

14 UCAF Raptors and 2 Chinese bombers were shot down during the raid.

Figure 14 - People's Republic of China tank crews assembling near Blythe, California, February 4, 2042. Image courtesy 中华人民共和国 美国冲突博物馆 *(People's Republic of China - American Conflict Museum in Beijing).*

By February 3, with Chinese ground forces overrunning its city garrison, ISSA Central Committee leaders fled San Francisco to a remote regional command center near Medford, Oregon.

On February 8, word reached the committee leaders in Medford of the surrender of all Mexican forces and the signing of the Treaty of Hermosillo. Under the treaty, the Mexican government denounced its earlier Declaración de San Jacinto and recognized the Ft. Bragg Congress as the sole legitimate government.

In exchange for a promise to not pursue punitive military action against Mexico, the Mexican government ceded the states of Baja California, Baja California Sur, Sonora, Chihuahua, and the northern half of Coahuila to the UCF.

Nine days later, on February 17, 2042, ISSA Central Committee leaders received word of the surrender of its remaining Western Command forces to Chinese air and ground units near Blythe, California. With the exception of troops occupying Davis-Monthan AFB near Tucson, Mountain Home AFB in Idaho, and assorted city garrisons, there remained no significant ISSA military forces in the west.

Seattle, Washington was in flames, and its mayor and the regional ISSA commander were last seen fleeing north to Canada.

Portland, Oregon's garrison commander had surrendered to the approaching Chinese forces. The state's ISSA-appointed governor, however, and several key members of her staff, fled to the governor's residence at Mahonia Hall in Salem and committed suicide.

In the south, Los Angeles was overrun by nearly 600,000 Chinese troops, and uncounted thousands of undocumented foreign nationals and other ISSA supporters were reportedly fleeing south towards Mexico.

San Francisco, ISSA's western capital, was a smoldering ruin, having been struck by 5 UCF B-83 nuclear bombs; the only city specifically targeted for nuclear destruction by the UCF during the conflict.

Western Holocaust

When the Chinese forces began landing on the west coast on January 1, 2042, ISSA Central Committee representatives in Ottawa, Canada sought an emergency meeting with the International Nuclear Force Commission (INFC).

At that meeting, ISSA representatives claimed to have achieved de-facto military victory in the conflict before so-called Chinese "interference" and demanded the INFC recognize ISSA as the legitimate government. The representatives also demanded the INFC release the country's nuclear launch codes to the ISSA Central Committee, in order to repel China's "foreign invasion".

The INFC refused, pointing to ISSA's recent defeats in the eastern region as evidence contradicting its claims of a decisive military victory. The committee also noted ISSA's own alliance with a foreign nation (Mexico), who had also crossed the country's border. Declaring the conflict "unresolved", the INFC refused to release the launch codes.

On February 19, 2042, in an act of incomprehensible hatred and spite, the ISSA Central Committee leaders at Medford ordered the detonation of 278 B-83 and B-61 nuclear warheads previously placed in strategic cities, military bases, and transportation hubs throughout the western states. The warheads had been carefully concealed in industrial metal drums packed with large quantities of cesium-137. When detonated, the massive "dirty bombs" scattered radioactive fallout and cesium dust far beyond the initial blast zones.

An estimated 19.4 million people were immediately killed in the denotations. 46.5 million more died within 3 years from related injuries, radiation, or cesium poisoning.

Chinese forces in the region suffered an estimated 642,000 casualties and immediately withdrew to evacuation ships hastily dispatched by Beijing and other sympathetic nations.

In total, the Western Holocaust, as the nuclear detonations were later called, directly contributed to more than 67 million deaths, and rendered the western region of the former USA uninhabitable for more than 30 years.

Figure 15 - Hispanic child in the ruins of Glendale, California, following multiple B-61 nuclear detonations in the Los Angeles area. Photo taken evening of March 04, 2042, by Maj James Renfro, UCF Nuclear Emergency Response Team Leader. Image courtesy Scherer American Conflict Museum, Pittsburgh PA, NAFS. File Number 1288B.

Historians consider the nuclear detonations on February 19, 2042, to be the official end of the American Conflict.

Aftermath (2042 – 2052)

23 of the 31 ISSA Central Committee members known to have been at Medford, Oregon on February 19, 2042, were ultimately arrested in Canada or the eastern states. Most had concealed themselves among the millions of refugees fleeing the western contamination.

Figure 16 - UCF Nuclear Emergency Response technician Cpl J. K. Palmer measuring cesium radiation levels in El Centro, California, April 2, 2042. Image courtesy Scherer American Conflict Museum, Pittsburgh PA, NAFS. File Number 1680G.

The bodies of 8 Central Committee members were found inside the Medford complex, having committed suicide after issuing the detonation orders.

4 of the 23 captured Central Committee leaders committed suicide following their arrest, but the remaining 19 survived to stand trial for war crimes at the 2045 Provisional NAFS War Crimes Tribunal in Ft. Benning, Georgia. All 19 were found guilty and hanged *(See: Provisional NAFS War Crimes Tribunal; NAFS-Archive Unit 09, 3s - (ar) 2082, Summary File: ED712BAA2E).*

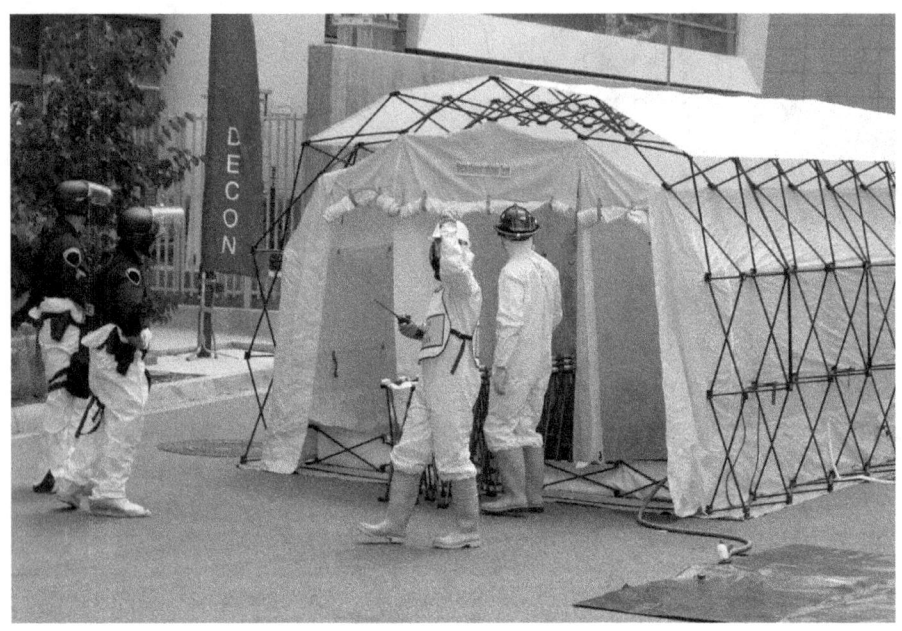

Figure 17 - Emergency decontamination station, Denver, Colorado, May 18, 2042. Photo taken by Sgt Jaden Marek, UCF Emergency Response. Image courtesy Scherer American Conflict Museum, Pittsburgh PA, NAFS. File Number 2310G.

For their part in ordering the burning deaths of 474 captured UCF officers inside the former U.S. Capitol Building, ISSA Central Committee Attaché Cassandra Cortez and Eastern Regional ISSA Commander Marco Isaacson were convicted of war crimes. They were transported, along with the prison commandant, to the former Joint Base Andrews UCF Prison, and executed by a firing squad composed of former camp prisoners.

The 628 known surviving members of ISSA's former North-Western Command were also arrested and charged with war crimes for their part in the unit's massacres in Idaho and Utah. 121 members of the group were hanged or executed by firing squad. The remaining 507 members received prison sentences ranging from 20 years to life, followed by expulsion from the country upon their release.

ISSA Central Committee Attaché Katherine Wyden, who had abandoned ISSA's North-Western Command when the force retreated from Utah, was discovered living with a sympathetic family in Orem, who believed her to be simply a displaced refugee from Ogden. Following her war crimes trial, Wyden was transported to the main Idahoan refugee settlement in Iowa and hanged in front of a delegation of Boise survivors.

The first legislation passed by the Ft. Bragg Congress following the nuclear detonations was the Treason Act of 2043. As proposed by the Provisional NAFS War Crimes Tribunal, the Treason Act authorized the arrest of all former Democratic Socialist Party leaders, all former house representatives who voted for the 2040 Electoral Suspension Act, all ISSA Central Committee members, and all ISSA regional governors and military commanders.

Those not convicted and executed for war crimes were stripped of their citizenship and property and expelled from the country. When Canada refused them entry, most relocated to France, Germany, Mexico, Columbia, Venezuela, Ecuador, El Salvador, or Argentina.

On July 4, 2048, amid great pomp and celebration, the Ft. Bragg Congress returned to the newly restored capitol building in Washington D.C.

The Ft. Bragg Congress served as the sole federal legislative body until the first post-conflict congressional primaries were held in 2052. During its brief tenure, the Ft. Bragg Congress passed numerous acts that dramatically changed the socio-political landscape of the new country.

Its first action in the new capitol building was to call for a re-vote on the Electoral Suspension Act of 2040. The act was read verbatim before the assembled lawmakers and a re-vote proposed. Then, following an emotional and stirring account of the recent conflict by Speaker of the House Martin Cooper, the body voted unanimously to reject the measure amid cheers from the assembled visitors.

Noting the hundreds of UCF officers who had been burned to death in that very room, Cooper then invited House Chaplain David Jones to offer a prayer on behalf of those who had died during the conflict.

The lawmakers then voted and sustained a proposition renaming the country the North America Federated States (NAFS), and set a date for a new presidential election the following year.

Under the Hermosillo Act of 2048, the Ft. Bragg Congress granted NAFS citizenship to any persons residing within those northern Mexican states acquired under the Treaty of Hermosillo, provided they signed the NAFS Allegiance Statement, completed a civics course, and renounced their Mexican citizenship. Representative and senatorial seats were also allocated to the new states and a congressional election date scheduled for six months following the presidential election.

In accordance with the provisions of the Sino Compact of 2041, the Ft. Bragg Congress withdrew the NAFS from the former United Nations on November 9, 2048.

Figure 18 - Santa Cruz, California. Photo taken by NAFS Radiological Survey Team on October 2, 2059. The city was heavily contaminated with cesium and abandoned following ISSA nuclear detonations in nearby San Jose and Salinas. Image courtesy Scherer American Conflict Museum, Pittsburgh PA, NAFS. File Number 9388J.

Following China and Great Britain's subsequent withdrawal the following year, the United Nations dissolved on December 5, 2049.

Under the Repatriation Act of 2050, all former ISSA service members below the rank of commander, who signed the NAFS Allegiance Statement, completed a mandatory civics course, and could prove they had been legal citizens of the (former) USA prior to January 2041, were repatriated as citizens of the NAFS. Those refusing or unable to meet the requirements were expelled from the country.

Figure 19 - Radioactive warning sign near Reno, Nevada, April 19, 2061. Photo taken by NAFS Radiological Survey Team. Image courtesy Scherer American Conflict Museum, Pittsburgh PA, NAFS. File Number 6637T.

Following the conflict, it was discovered that large numbers of ISSA's forces, particularly its ground forces, were comprised of undocumented foreign nationals. By some estimates, as many as 22% of the ISSA Western and North-Western Command forces were foreign nationals who had been either residing in the country without proper authorization or had entered the country immediately following the outbreak of hostilities to support the socialist regime.

Under the North America Federated States Defense Act of 2051 (NAFSDA), unauthorized entry into the country, as well as unauthorized residence within the country, was redefined as a military attack upon the nation's sovereignty.

Persons over the age of 18 arrested under the Act were subjected to a military tribunal and, if convicted, sentenced to 20 years of hard labor followed by expulsion back to their country of origin. Those convicted of a second offense were designated as hostile foreign insurgents and subject to military execution.

Persons under the age of 18 detained under the act were expelled back to their country of origin.

Under the NAFSDA, any NAFS citizen knowingly employing or harboring unauthorized foreign nationals within the country was subject to the same penalties.

As a result of NAFSDA, millions of unauthorized foreign nationals self-deported back to their respective countries, greatly alleviating the country's western refugee crisis following the nuclear holocaust.

ISSA's nuclear detonations contaminated vast areas of the west with cesium-137, rendering the region uninhabitable. The areas most affected were California, Oregon, Washington, Arizona, Nevada, Utah, and Idaho (formerly USA), Baja California and western Sonora (formerly Mexico), and southwestern British Columbia (Canada).

One of the last acts passed by the Ft. Bragg Congress was the Resettlement Ban of 2052. Under the ban, entry into the western NAFS was restricted to scientific and environmental inspection teams. The ban remained in effect until 2073, when the cesium had decayed sufficiently to permit resettlement of the region.

Though short in duration, the American Conflict resulted in

more than 67 million deaths, making it the deadliest conflict in world history.

End Summary File: EF8FAD856//:QKDS-51676F54

The Luyteni

Begin Summary File: A942B127BA//:QKDS-51676F54A

Luyten's Star (GJ-273)

Luyten's Star (GJ-273) is a V magnitude 9.87, or "red dwarf" star located in the constellation of Canis Minor, approximately 1.2 light years from Procyon, and 12.36 light years from Earth.

The star was named "Luyten's Star" after its discoverer, Dutch-American astronomer Willem Jacob Luyten (1899-1994). Luyten and his colleague, Edwin G. Ebbighausen (1911-1984) began studying the star in 1935 because of its high proper motion of 3.7 arc seconds per year.

The star is approximately 29.3% the size of our own star, Sol, with a surface temperature only 58.5% of ours, making Luyten's star both smaller and cooler than our own.

The innermost planet, Luyten Minor (GJ-273c), is 1.18 times larger than Earth, with a comparable surface gravity. The planet orbits very close to its star, completing one orbit every 4.72 days, and its surface temperature ranges from a blistering 53.83°C to an absolutely deadly 188.85°C.

Luyten Minor's atmosphere is composed of carbon dioxide (94%), nitrogen (5%), and various other trace gases. While it may have had a thicker atmosphere at one time, the planet's weak magnetic field and close proximity to its star have resulted in most of its heavier gases being stripped away by stellar activity.

Luyten Minor shares spin-orbital resonance with Luyten Major and has a planetary rotation of 28.4 hours.

The Luyteni homeworld, Luyten Major (GJ-273b), is the

second planet in the Luyteni star system. The planet is approximately 2.89 times larger than our Earth and orbits its star every 18.65 days. The planet's gravity is approximately 1.6 times that of Earth's, and its surface temperature ranges from a frigid minus 67.15°C at its poles, to a very comfortable 19.85°C at its equatorial region.

Though its star is considerably less bright than our sun, the relative close orbit of the planet to its star results in it receiving 6% more of its star's light than the Earth receives from its sun.

Luyten Major's atmosphere is similar to Earth's, consisting of nitrogen (72%), oxygen (25%), carbon dioxide (1%) argon (0.84%), ozone (0.14%), and traces of other gases, including large quantities of water vapor. Luyten Major also has a strong magnetic field, shielding the planet from adverse stellar activity.

Approximately 58% of Luyten Major is ocean, with the remaining planet consisting of vast forests in its warmer regions with artic plains in its extreme latitudes. Luyten Major shares spin-orbital resonance with Luyten Minor and has a planetary rotation of 31.34 hours.

The third planet (GJ-273d) is a small planet, approximately 0.32 times the size of our Earth. A dim, meteor impacted body devoid of atmosphere, it has 1 large moon, approximately .42 times the size of the planet itself. The planet and its moon are tidally locked, and orbit around the star every 422.3 days at a 9.4-degree tilt from the star's equator.

The fourth planet (GJ-273e) is another cold, small planet, approximately 0.52 times the size of the Earth, slightly smaller than our Mars. This dark, frozen planet has a thin atmosphere composed primarily of carbon dioxide, with traces of nitrogen. The planet reportedly has 6 moons and orbits its star every 704.9 days

2017 Tromsø Signal

On October 16, 17, and 18, 2017, a binary-encoded radio signal was transmitted from a 32m European Incoherent Scatter Scientific Association (EISCAT) radio antenna located in Tromsø, Norway. The signal, transmitted using a binary system of two alternating frequencies pulsing at 125 times per second, was directed towards Luyten's Star.

```
010011000111000001111100000000111111100000000000011111111111
011111111111111111000000000000000000000111111111111111111100
110000000000000000000000000000000111111111111111111111111111
111111111111111111111100000000000000000000000000000000000000
000000000000000000000000000000000000000111111111111111111111
000000000000000000000111111111111111111111111111111111111111
000000000000111111111111111111111111111111111111111111111111
000000000000111111111111111111111111111111111111111111111111
000000000000000000000000111111111111111111111111111111111111
```

Figure 20 - Binary segment from October 16, 2017, Tromsø, Norway EISCAT radio signal to GJ-273b (Luyten's Star).

The Luyten's star project, known as "Sónar Calling GJ 273b", was a collaboration involving METI International - the Institute of Space Studies of Catalonia in Spain, and Sónar, a music, creativity, and technology festival in Barcelona, Spain.

The signal itself consisted of little more than a scientific and mathematical tutorial on how to decode the messages, accompanied by 33 encoded musical compositions by various musicians.

A second signal series was transmitted on May 14, 15, and 16, 2018.

2046 Luyteni Signal

On June 9, 2046, while analyzing the stellar spectrum of Luyten's star (GJ-273), the PRL Advance Radial-velocity Abu-sky Search (PARAS) spectrograph at the Guru Shikhar Observatory in Mount Abu, Rajasthan, Sirohi district, India, detected an extremely complex repeating series of 8 light pulses of the order of 10^{-15} s, with varying time separations, superimposed against the star's visible spectrum.

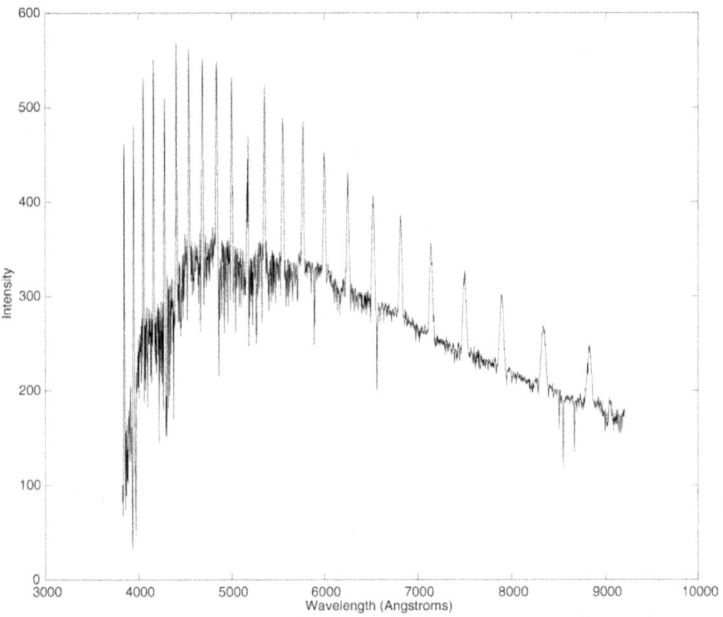

Figure 21 - 2036 Luyteni signal sequence, showing 8 pulses (N = 8) and τ = 5 × 10^{-15} s superposed against the spectrum of Luyten's star (GJ-273), after applying Fourier transformation of the frequency spectrum.

The light pulses, separated by apparently random time sequences ranging from τ_1 to τ_9, were clearly artificially produced and directed towards the Earth.

The pulses appeared to follow no discernible pattern, other than being 22 distinct pattern sequences, each separated by 2.35-hour pauses. The entire series duration was 204.82 hours and was repeated every 18.65 days; the known orbital cycle of the second exoplanet in the Luyten star system.

While it was not known how long the pulses had been transmitting before their initial detection, the entire series ceased after 362.55 days, constituting 19 serial repetitions of the 22 complete pulse sequences, plus the initial sequence group recorded mid-series.

The signals stunned the world and exhilarated the scientific community. However, despite massive research expenditures by virtually every technologically-advanced nation, scientists could not decipher the signals.

The following year, beginning on May 4, 2047, a second series of signals was detected. Like the first, it consisted of multiple serial repetitions, repeating every 18.65 days.

Each year thereafter, a new series was detected.

On October 2, 2047, while analyzing a computer simulation of human brain neuron activity, Dr. Tatsuya Kuyama, Deputy Director at the RIKEN Center for Advanced Intelligence Project in Japan, observed the timing delays inherent to brain neuron firing patterns were similar to the timing differentials discovered within the Luyten spectra pulse signals.

After consulting with Dr. Toshiro Yamada, Senior Advisor at the RIKEN Center for Advanced Photonics, the researchers approached the Fujitsu Quantum Computing (QCOMP) group in Tokyo.

After nearly 10 months, QCOMP researchers were able to construct an interpretive modeling program for the Luyten pulse signal. The signals, they discovered, were visual representations of Luyteni cognitive brain wave patterns, represented as time-varying pulsations of visible light. The Luyteni were quite literally "sharing their thoughts" with the Earth.

The first series' sequence was discovered to represent a pattern of binary numbers and simple mathematic equations. Using those sequences as a primer, the researchers were able to extrapolate additional translations from the increasingly-complex pulse sequences.

Within a month, the Fujitsu QCOMP computer model had successfully translated color spectra, geometric shapes, periodic table elements, time, and distance measurements. Within a year, all 22 of the first series had been translated.

On May 16, 2049, the RIKEN researchers published the Luyteni messages to a shocked world. (*See: "The Luyteni Coda"; NAFS-Archive Unit 75, 12p - (ar) 2055, (r-ar) 2125, File: 2E98C4E3CB*).

While the distance between the two star systems results in a nearly 25-year delay between question and answer, once the Luyteni received man's subsequent response, they increased the number of unique signals transmitted to the Earth and decreased the interval between each distinct series.

In the more than 100 years since translating the first Luyteni signal, the Earth has received more than 1,320 distinct TVS pulse communications from the Luyteni.

The information the Luyteni have chosen to share with the Earth suggests they are an extremely peaceful, friendly civilization, eager to share their knowledge with man (*See: "Plus de Silence" – by Adrien Dessele; NAFS-Archive Unit 75, 18j - (ar) 2059, File: 215C3D8452*).

Luyteni Civilization

The Luyteni are a scientifically-advanced civilization rating approximately .9633 on the revised Kardashev-Kovic scale of civilization development. By this measurement, the Luyteni civilization is approximately 1,147 (± 8.6) years ahead of our own, which in 2148 rated .7518 on the same scale.

The Luyteni civilization consumes nearly 92% of the energy reaching its planet, approximately 94,330 exajules, or 2,991.18 terawatts of energy.

By comparison, humanity's total energy consumption in the year 2148 was 3,840 exajules, or 121.77 terawatts.

The Luyteni homeworld, Luyten Major, (GJ-273b), is ringed by a massive solar energy collection array. The array is maintained in a low heliosynchronous orbit around the planet, at a surface altitude of approximately 1,540km. Completed more than 400 years ago, the array produces approximately 74% of the total energy consumed by the Luyteni civilization.

Unlike the palladium micro-alloy glass nano-threaded lifts mankind used to connect to its early low-orbital platforms, the heliosynchronous orbit of the Luyteni e-ring made it impossible for the Luyteni to connect the ring directly to their planet's surface. In addition, being on a planet with a heavier gravity than ours, the Luyteni faced considerable challenges placing objects of significant mass into orbit.

Following their discovery of transitional phased-matter singularities approximately 510 years ago, the Luyteni civilization was able to overcome the gravitational problems inherent in the construction of such a monumental orbital structure. However, even with such tools, the Luyteni reportedly took 36 years to complete their first circumferential ring *(See: "The Luyteni E-Ring"; NAFS-Archive Unit 75, 28f - (ar) 2105, File: 237DA24B7D).*

The Luyteni maintain 134 sealed artificial "micro-moon" structures orbiting their home planet. The massive sealed spherical structures, some more than 43km in diameter, are used for scientific research and advanced substrate manufacturing and are accessed via calibrated phased-matter singularities. The Luyteni spectra pulse signals are reportedly broadcast to Earth from one of these micro-moon structures, as the orbit of Luyten Major brings the structure within line-of-sight to Earth every 18.65 days *(See: "The Micro-Moons of Luyten Major"; NAFS-Archive Unit 75, 19w - (ar) 2101, File: 61AAD5A34A).*

The Luyteni operate mining facilities on Luyten Minor (GJ-273c), their closest planetary neighbor and their system's innermost planet. Due to Luyten Minor's extreme surface temperature, the mines are constructed entirely underground and are restricted to geographic latitudes between 90°N and 30°N, and 90°S and 30°S.

The spatial limitations of quantum-entangled phased-matter make it impossible for the Luyteni to transit directly from Luyten Major to Luyten Minor. The Luyteni maintain a network of orbiting singularity platforms to facilitate transit and shipping between the two planets, similar to those that man has deployed between the Earth and Mars.

The primary elements mined on Luyten Minor are indium, tellurium, boron, osmium, cadmium, dysprosium, neodymium, gallium, and molybdenum. The minerals are transported via calibrated singularities to Luyten Major, or to manufacturing facilities within the Luyteni micro-moon structures *(See: "Luyteni Mining" – by Cabot Bourreau; NAFS-Archive Unit 72, 11v - (ar) 2098, File: 93611E7EAB).*

Due to its proximity to its star, and its heavy surface gravity, Luyten Major is extraordinarily flat in comparison to Earth. Oceans cover approximately 58% of the Luyteni home planet. Nearly 96% of the planet's remaining terrestrial biosphere is cultivated, developed, or otherwise controlled by the Luyteni.

Figure 22 - Artist rendition of a Luyteni city, "Luyten Morning" by Elisa Badeau (2033 - 2104). Image courtesy New Metropolitan Museum of Art, New York.

Agricultural development encompasses approximately 24% of the available terrestrial surface. Manufacturing, industrial, and energy production utilize approximately 42% of the surface. The remaining 32% is covered by mega-city population centers. The Luyteni live in extremely large cities, with more than 20 million occupants being common. The Luyteni also maintain numerous floating ocean-city complexes, as well as vast aquatic bio-agricultural facilities.

Sociologists believe the Luyteni civilization to be heavily

automated, far more than our own. Virtually every aspect of the Luyteni civilization appears to be supported by automata, robotics, or what mankind calls self-directed control units. The rare-earth elements mined on Luyten Minor, and their vast energy consumption, support this supposition.

The bulk of the Luyteni manufacturing facilities, both on their home planet and their orbiting micro-moons, appear to be dedicated to either power generation or automata production *(See: "Estimativa de Automação Luyteni" – Ministério de Ciência, Tecnologia, Inovação, Comunicações e Automação (Brasil); NAFS-Archive Unit 112, 44z - (ar) 2101, File: D50475862A).*

Luyteni Biology

The Luyteni are a semi-bipedal, carbon-based, intelligent exo-lifeform.

Shorter than humans, the average height of a Luyteni, when standing erect, is 131cm. Like humans, the Luyteni are covered with a contiguous integumentary skin, surrounding internal organs and a dense bone structure.

The heavy gravity of Luyten Major has greatly influenced Luyteni skeletal and musculature development, resulting in thick, heavy muscles and extremely strong, dense bones. Luyteni bones have high concentrations of manganese, copper, and boron. Biologists believe it unlikely the Luyteni ever suffer from accidental bone breaks, even when falling from a considerable height. In addition, the Luyteni preferred method of locomotion, a semi-bipedal gait supported by their long arms, appears to greatly reduce both the risk of a fall, while also minimizing injuries sustained should such a fall occur.

In addition to short, extremely muscular legs, the Luyteni have two muscular arms that reach almost to the surface when standing erect. Both the legs and the arms are dual-jointed, though the joints on the Luyteni legs are closely spaced, almost fused, giving the appearance of a single 'knee' joint. The Luyteni arms are jointed at intervals between their thoracic connection and their hands, and this provides their arms with great flexibility of movement.

The Luyteni feet are flat, pad structures, with four small vestigial toes, mere bumps on the front and side of their thickly-muscled feet. Evolved for stability and strong forward pushing movement, the Luyteni feet are supported by very thick bone joints and sinews.

At the end of their arms, the Luyteni have hand-type appendages, with four extremely long and agile fingers measuring almost 20cm in length, each with 4 separate knuckle joints. When "walking", a Luyteni's hands are folded under its palms, reminiscent of an ape walking on its knuckles.

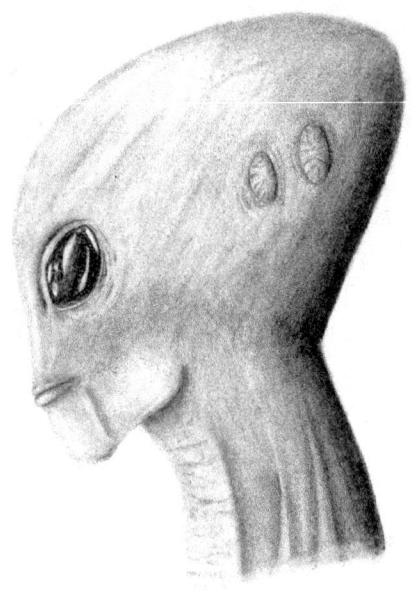

Figure 23 – Luyteni sketch by Copernicus City Primary student, Jayme Wilkins, Luna Talent Exhibition, February 2144.

The Luyteni brain is a four-lobed structure encased within an elongated skeletal shell of considerable thickness. The lobes of the Luyteni brain are hemispherically-locked, connecting to a central brain stem that branches rapidly into neuro-connective tissues similar to nerves. The Luyteni have no spine. Instead, their frame is supported by dense bone segments protecting vital organs, connected by considerable internal musculature and tendons.

Like man, the Luyteni are omnivorous, though they have lower protein and higher mineral dietary requirements than man.

The Luyteni have two large black eyes, placed forward on their skulls, providing them with excellent distance vision.

The Luyteni have no nose in the conventional sense. However, they do have olfactory openings located under their chin, as well as secondary olfactory glands located just inside their mouth.

The Luyteni have two sets of tympanic membranes located on either side of their elongated cranium for auditory reception.

Evolution Influences

The Luyteni report they evolved from a hairless sloth-like creature in the ancient primordial forests of their planet. Due to Luyten Major's heavy gravity, this proto-luyteni ancestor built plant and rock "nests" on the forest floor rather than in the canopy of the trees. The Luyteni credit this ancient nesting construction as the catalyst for their eventual tool development.

While Luyten Major actually receives 6% more light from its star than the Earth receives from its sun, the thick surface mists and dense forest cover of the planet have resulted in the Luyteni being more sensitive to bright light than man. The Luyteni are most active in the early dawn and late dusk hours while preferring to rest during the brightest and hottest hours of their day.

Like man, the Luyteni have bi-ocular vision, but the large, black Luyteni eyes have evolved to capture a wider wavelength spectrum than man's, varying into the infrared. Luyteni vision processes light wavelengths from about 460 to more than 980 nanometers. By contrast, human eyes process light wavelengths from about 390 to only 700 nanometers.

Figure 24 - Recreation of a Luyteni forest from "The Luyteni Exhibit" at the National Science Gallery in London, circa 2142. Image courtesy The National Science Gallery, London, UK.

Their ability to see into the infrared undoubtedly helped the Luyteni's proto-ancestors avoid predators as well as locate prey in the dark primordial forest.

The Luyteni's incredibly sensitive auditory and olfactory organs undoubtedly developed for the same purpose; to allow their ancestors to avoid noisy predators and seek elusive prey in the dark forest.

The Luyteni "ears" are reportedly more sensitive than a

cat's and can distinguish sounds between 8Hz – 64,000Hz. By comparison, humans can hear sounds between 20Hz to 20,000Hz.

The Luyteni report being able to smell certain plant growths more than a meter under the forest floor, or an animal more than 22 kilometers away, suggesting their sense of smell may be as sensitive as the Earth's bear.

Communication and Writing

The Luyteni's dim forest origins also contributed to the development of their extraordinary method of communication.

The Luyteni's integumentary skin consists of a thin, semi-transparent membrane surrounding a layer of chromatophoric pigment cells. The pigment cells allow the Luyteni to rapidly change their skin color and patterns to precisely mimic their surroundings.

Undoubtedly evolved as concealment from predators in the ancient primordial forests, the Luyteni are masters of camouflage, exceeding even the remarkable abilities of our own Earth's octopus and cuttlefish. The Luyteni use their incredible chromatophoric capability to communicate, expressing their thoughts and even their moods, as brilliant pulsations of color and patterns on their skin. What a Luyteni is thinking can quite literally be seen on their skin. This chromatophoric skin-based communication is the primary reason why the Luyteni wear no clothing. The Luyteni supplement this extraordinary visual communication with a complex pattern of audible clicks, whistles, and breaths.

The Luyteni developed a written language more than eight thousand years ago, rendering their visual and auditory communication into a graceful, flowing script.

Some linguists have argued that the Luyteni method of communication is actually superior to man's; in that the Luyteni's chromatophoric language is capable of more accurately representing mood, emotion, and intensity of feeling, with fewer language constructions *(See: "Luyteni Sprachentwicklung: Eine Kritische Analyse" – by Robert Wilhelm; NAFS-Archive Unit 14, 10d - (ar) 2084, File: 110F90282E).*

The Luyteni have no music and the concept of music is foreign to them. When the Luyteni received mankind's original Tromsø signal and its accompanying musical compositions, they recognized it as being sent from an intelligent species but were confused as to the message's meaning.

Lacking their own musical corollary, the Luyteni misinterpreted the auditory waveform patterns as some form of emotive communication. Curiously, the Luyteni report being aware of some of the "feelings" invoked by the musical compositions, but were confused as to their ultimate meaning.

When they constructed their response, the Luyteni simply converted their own pulsing chromatophoric thoughts into light spectra waveforms, and then directed the patterns towards the Earth.

Genome and Procreation

The Luyteni genome is based on micro-beaded TNA, or threose nucleic acid. Unlike human DNA, the Luyteni genetic structure maintained its early TNA origins, evolving from primitive tertiary folding shapes with discrete ligand-binding properties, into its present 4-strand interlocking beaded threads. While each TNA bead carries only 18 molecules, the interlocked 4-strand arrangement results in an astounding 68,719,476,736 possible combinations. Thus, while the Luyteni have less basic genetic material to work with, they actually have a more-genetically diverse population than mankind's.

Geneticists believe the Luyteni genome evolved in this way due to higher levels of stellar radiation reaching their early planet when the planet's sun was brighter, resulting in the need for micro-organisms in the planet's early oceans and forests to diversify or go extinct during periods of increased stellar activity *(See: "A Study of the Luyteni Genome" – Dr. Sabrina Braden, University of Cambridge, Department of Genetics; NAFS-Archive Unit 79, 115w - (ar) 2110, File: 0DD305484A).*

The Luyteni live to an average age of 47 years. The Luyteni reproduce sexually, are non-monogamous, and are oviparous. While all Luyteni are capable of reproduction by 3 years of age, less than 14% of the population actually produce offspring. Conception may involve as few as two, to more than ten different Luyteni, and any or all of those involved may ultimately produce young.

Between 2 and 4 eggs are typically laid in a single clutch, but clutches of 1 or more than 4 eggs can also occur. As with some animals on Earth, the number of eggs laid in a clutch appears to be influenced by environment, stress, and other factors. The eggs are cared for by the nesting Luyteni. While fertilization may utilize genetic information contributed by multiple Luyteni, all of the eggs in a single Luyteni clutch are genetically identical to each other. Eggs are laid within 12 days of fertilization, and incubation of the eggs takes 6.26 earth months. Following birth, the immature Luyteni are cared for by the community at-large and abandoned by their biological progenitors. A breeding Luyteni typically lays between 6 to 8 egg clutches during their lifetime.

The concept of familial care of offspring seems foreign to the

Luyteni, though they report the behavior is evident in some of their planet's fauna.

End Summary File: A942B127BA//:QKDS-51676F54A

The Exotic Phased-Matter Singularity

Begin Summary File: 850DC689DD//:QKDS-51676F54A

P-SEQS

Perhaps no contribution by the Luyteni has had a greater impact on mankind than the exotic phased-matter singularity.

The Luyteni's 9th signal series, received in March 2055, contained technical and scientific information that allowed mankind to begin construction of its first exotic phased matter (EPM) containment facility.

Construction and Management

Construction began in February 2056 near Geneva, Switzerland under a development agreement between the former German, French, and Switzerland governments.

The project, named Projet de Singularité Enchevêtrée Quantique Stabilisée (P-SEQS), or "Stabilized Quantum Entangled Singularity Project", became the primary consumer of mankind's scientific and technical efforts for more than a decade.

Management of the P-SEQS project was shared between the venerable Conseil Européen pour la Recherche Nucléaire (CERN or "European Council for Nuclear Research"), and the former German government's Bundesanstalt für Materialforschung und Prüfung (the "Federal Institute for Materials Research and Testing").

Cost

Constructed on land reclaimed from the National Nature Reserve on the French side of the border with Geneva, the cost of the project was enormous. Over a 10-year period, P-SEQS cost an estimated 20.2 trillion euros, or more than 35% of the combined gross domestic product output of Germany, France, and Switzerland during those years.

Factoring in the additional development and manufacturing costs of the more than 30 supporting nations, the project was the among the costliest construction efforts in mankind's history, second only to the Arch-Gale colony on Mars *(See: "P-SEQS: Kostenanalyse" - Konföderation der Germanischen Staaten Budget und Buchhaltungsbüro; NAFS-Archive Unit 8, 11h - (ar) 2123, File: F539339DB0)*.

Power Generation

Powering the P-SEQS facility was a major problem in the early days of fusion. The former governments of Germany, France, and Switzerland were forced to rely on older nuclear power to create the first singularity.

When construction of the facility began in 2056, nearly 48 square kilometers were set aside for power generation. European, Chinese, and Japanese companies were solicited to construct what would ultimately become the world's largest nuclear power facility.

The North America Federated States, still recovering from the devastating American Conflict, did not participate in the P-SEQS project until 2062, when Massachusetts-based General Electric company secured the contract to supply the facility's array of 60Hz turbine generators.

When construction of the power facility was finally completed in 2064, its 36 pressurized water reactors, each with the capacity to produce 1.5 gigawatts of electric power, produced so much steam during operation that it affected local weather patterns in nearby Geneva.

The facility was capable of evaporating up to 912,000,000 cubic meters of water each year from nearby Lake Geneva and was the largest single European power supplier during those periods when the P-SEQS facility was not engaged in active testing.

Collider

The most important structure within the 100-square kilometer P-SEQS facility was the collider building. This building housed the control center, the EPM containment unit, the tunneling regulator platform, and a third generation KEK-GenQ quantum-TeV ion accelerator.

The original CERN Large Hadron Collider (LHC) in Geneva (circa 2008 – 2036) used a 27-kilometer ring of superconducting magnets, with assorted accelerating plants along its circumference that boosted particle energy as they traversed the ring. The LHC could take up to 90 minutes to accelerate a particle stream, typically achieving 7 trillion electron volts (TeV), or 0.99999999 c (the speed of light).

By comparison, the KEK-GenQ accelerator, manufactured by the High-Energy Accelerator Corporation in Ibaraki, Japan, was a mere 46-meters in length, yet was capable of accelerating positively charged osmium ions within its polarized QED vacuum to an astonishing 2,097.94 trillion electron volts (TeV) in a mere 14.2 seconds, or 0.9999999999999 c (speed of light); more than 100,000 times faster than the older LHC.

EPM Containment Unit

It was clear from the Luyteni design models, that a quantum-entangled phased matter singularity, once created, could only be contained within a containment unit of an incredibly dense ionically-charged material capable of superconducting under varying temperatures.

Figure 25 - P-SEQS KEK-GenQ quantum-TeV ion accelerator, April, 2064. Image courtesy High-Energy Accelerator Corporation.

In 2062, by following the substrate manufacturing techniques provided by the Luyteni, researchers working within the Department of Materials Engineering at the University of Tokyo successfully synthesized partially electron-depleted osmium from osmium-192.

The ionized osmium, now at 102.42 grams per cubic centimeter, was the densest material ever created, and at 502 gigapascals, was harder than a diamond. With more than half of its electrons removed, the depleted osmium also had an extremely strong positive ionic charge.

The depleted osmium EPM containment unit at the original P-SEQS facility was more than 1.5 meters in diameter and weighed more than 350 kilograms. By contrast, EPM containment devices today are typically less than 15 centimeters in diameter and weigh less than 4 kilograms.

Manufactured for P-SEQS by the University of Tokyo, it was the only tier-1 component not produced by a commercial entity.

Tunneling Regulator

The original Luyteni EPM design did not include a tunneling regulator for temporal cycling. It wasn't until the Luyteni's 15th signal series, received in July 2059, that the concept of a tunneling regulator was first introduced. As a result, the original 2055 P-SEQS facility design did not make allowance for the addition of a tunneling regulator.

In 2066, the EPM collider floor, now nearing completion, was hastily modified to include a raised platform above the EPM containment unit for the tunneling regulator equipment.

The Luyteni design model specified the tunneling regulator's close proximity to the EPM containment unit, however, P-SEQS engineers were concerned that the regulator's nested superconducting electromagnetic spheres might adversely affect the tensor assembly's gravimetric field strength on the EPM containment unit.

To accommodate the engineer's concerns, the platform was constructed to permit the entire 5-tonne platform to be mechanically raised further away from the EPM containment unit if needed.

To their chagrin, the engineers later discovered the tunneling regulator's proximity to the EPM containment unit actually improved the tensor's overall field strength. Thus, rather than raising the regulator platform, the P-SEQS engineers actually lowered it until it was almost touching the top of the EPM's containment unit.

Figure 26 - P-SEQS tunneling regulator platform, June 2066, constructed on top of the EPM containment unit, looking down on the collider floor. Image courtesy P-SEQS History Museum in Geneva.

The platform's new position resulted in more than one head injury, and is the origin of the tunneling regulator's nickname among quantum engineers; the "knocker".

Stress-Energy Tensor

The tensor assembly facility, located immediately east of the P-SEQS collider building near the foot of the Crêt de la Neige mountain peak, was easily the most speculative of the project's many components.

Constructed by the National Physical Laboratory in London, UK, the tensor assembly's engineers were forced to improvise several of the facility's functions.

Based on certain omissions in the Luyteni signal designs, scientists realized that the Luyteni had a working understanding of both artificial and anti-gravity theory and that they had assumed mankind possessed a similar level of understanding.

This mistaken assumption on the part of the Luyteni presented the NPL tensor assembly team with serious challenges, as the Luyteni had neglected to document several key formulas in their tensor design instructions; most important of these being the energy density requirements for an object transiting the singularity's event horizon.

Although a response to the Luyteni signals had been sent in 2050, mankind would not receive a reply to that second signal until at least 2074. So, while the Luyteni were voluntarily sharing an incredible amount of scientific and theoretical information with the Earth, the NPL project engineers had no means of asking the Luyteni for immediate assistance with the stress-energy tensor problem.

From the Luyteni design specifications, the engineers were aware that an electromagnetic field properly interacting with a time-varying current would produce the gravimetric energy needed to sustain the space-time singularity's co-generation process. However, they were not provided with any details on calculating the null energy along on EPM singularity's event horizon during quantum coupling of the singularity's event horizons.

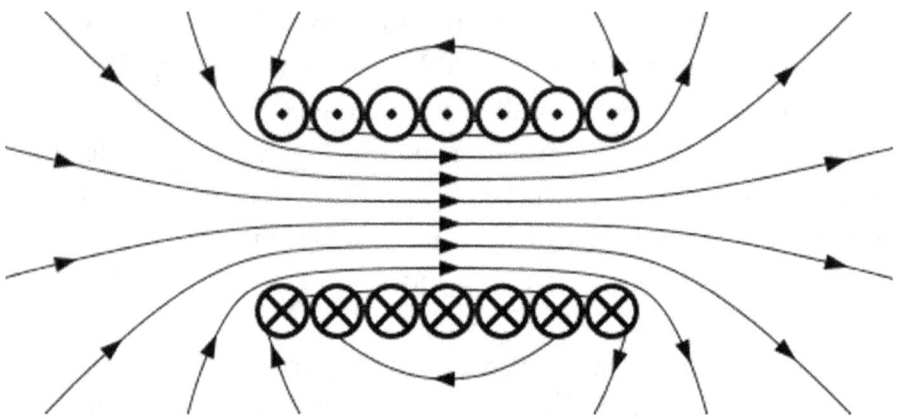

Figure 27 - Electromagnetic properties of stress-energy tensor. (Below) Dean's Formula, establishing null energy along the EPM singularity's event horizon remains positive, permitting transition:

$$\int_{U_0}^{\infty} dU\, T_{UU}$$

$$= -\frac{h\Gamma(2\Delta+1)^2}{2^{4\Delta}(2\Delta+1)\Gamma(\Delta)^2\Gamma(\Delta+1)^2\ell} \cdot \frac{{}_2F_1\left(\frac{1}{2}+\Delta, \frac{1}{2}-\Delta; \frac{3}{2}+\Delta; \frac{1}{1+U_0^2}\right)}{\left(1+U_0^2\right)^{\Delta+1/2}}$$

On May 12, 2064, Nigel Dean, a theoretical physicist employed at the National Physical Laboratory in London, announced he had resolved the tensor problem.

Dean had observed that, for all Δ values from 0 to 1, the integral of TUU was always negative, which confirmed the existence of a traversable singularity using his tensor model.

Unable to test the model except during actual operation, the National Physical Laboratory took a chance and constructed the tensor assembly according to Dean's formula. The entire unit was then disassembled, shipped, and reassembled on-site at the P-SEQS facility next to the EPM containment building.

On October 30, 2067, the date scheduled for the first singularity test, Dean and the NPL team waited anxiously on the collider floor. When the first test object, a tungsten icosahedron nodule, was successfully passed through the spatially-separated event horizons, the NPL team erupted in applause and cheers.

Dean was later presented with the nodule at his Nobel Prize award ceremony (*See: "Nigel Dean – a Biography" – by Susan Dean Gagne; NAFS-Archive Unit 91, 2q - (ar) 2090, File: C42CE31011*).

First Singularity

Mankind's first stabilized singularity was achieved on October 30, 2067, at the P-SEQS facility near Geneva, Switzerland.

The tensor calibration cycle lasted more than 31 hours and required 35.37 gigawatts of energy to generate the 2.5-meter singularity. Once generated, the EPM unit needed 1.3 gigawatts of energy to maintain the calibration.

By comparison, a 4-meter singularity today can be spatially-calibrated in a matter of seconds, typically requires less than 1 gigawatt to generate, and needs as little as 60 megawatts of energy to maintain.

Power Startup

At 02:30 on the morning of October 26, 2067, Ondrej Masarik, the Director-General of the P-SEQS project, issued the order for power startup of all reactors.

The 36 nuclear power plants immediately commenced their blow-down procedures, eliminating condensate from the reactor-farm's many steam-traps.

By 14:00 that afternoon, the Director of Power Operations, Ansel Von Kampen, signaled a "go for primary soak", permitting the miles of piping within the radioactive side of the reactor containment domes to be brought up to temperature.

At 10:30 on October 28, 2067, with all 36 primary reactors now at temperature, Von Kampen signaled "go for secondary soak", to permit the piping outside of the reactor domes to be brought up to temperature.

Within 30 minutes of that order, the P-SEQS communications building began notifying thousands of sponsors, contractors, and government officials to expect the first EPM calibration test to occur within 24 hours.

Figure 28 - Early Hitachi "Gen-D" SDUs monitoring the quantum control processors at the P-SEQS controller building, September 2066. Image courtesy Hitachi Robotics Corporation.

News and media organizations around the world immediately interrupted their programming to begin live streaming video of the nuclear farm's startup operations. Tens of thousands of spectators began gathering in the streets and on the rooftops in nearby Geneva, watching excitedly to the west for the characteristic steam plumes rising above the mountains that would indicate the power plants in operation.

Until this moment, the P-SEQS power facility had conducted only incremental startup drills of its 36 reactors, permitting groups of reactors to be brought to temperature, cycle for some period of time, inspected, and then allowed to cool down.

The facility's charter with the French, German, and Switzerland governments mandated no more than 9 of the 36 generators would be permitted to continually operate except during periods of EPM testing. Typically, no more than 6 P-SEQS reactors had been in operation at any point in time.

At 8:30 on October 29, 2067, Von Kampen signaled for the first time, "Go for power - all units".

In Geneva, crowds gasped in astonishment as a wall of white steam more than 12 kilometers wide appeared over the western mountains and began boiling upwards towards the heavens.

Reactor 22 Failure

At 09:12, control engineers monitoring reactor number 22 sounded an alarm. One of the high-pressure pipes outside of the reactor's radioactive containment unit had fractured. A control valve had failed to open, preventing the pipe from reaching temperature during its secondary soak procedure, and when subjected to high-pressure steam, the pipe had fractured explosively.

With a nuclear power alarm sounding in the P-SEQS operations room, Director General Masarik ordered all P-SEQS personnel to "hold pending shut down" and turned operational control over to Director of Power Operations, Ansel Von Kampen, according to the facility's nuclear emergency procedures.

In Geneva, the warning sirens coming from the distant P-SEQS complex less than an hour after the release of such an unprecedented steam cloud, alarmed many. Some spectators began to panic and more than a dozen people were injured attempting to jump down from their rooftop vantage points.

Within an hour, however, the problem had been identified, and Von Kampen ordered reactor 22 to begin cool down procedures. With reactor 22 safely shutting down, Von Kampen returned operational control to Masarik, who issued an "all clear" and ordered all personnel to resume preparations for calibration.

"Go for Calibration"

By 11:00 on October 29, 2067, with the 35 remaining reactors nearing 60% capacity, the facility was generating more than 31 gigawatts of power, a world record at that time for a single power facility.

By 12:30, Von Kampen signaled power levels had reached 35 gigawatts.

Finally, at 13:46, Von Kampen signaled the plant had reached the targeted 36.75 gigawatts of electrical generation.

Masarik sounded a single "warning" horn over the P-SEQS complex loudspeakers and ordered all personnel to their designated safety areas.

On the EPM collider floor, engineers made final checks on the floor's coiled quantum-TeV ion accelerator, and the EPM containment unit.

In the tensor building, the National Physical Laboratory team powered up its tensor assembly controller.

At 14:05, with all departments reporting "go" conditions, P-SEQS Director General Ondrej Masarik sounded a triple horn over the complex loudspeakers, followed by the order, "Go for calibration".

At the nearby transformer farm, hundreds of transformers engaged with a devastating snap, while in nearby Geneva, lights dimmed, fluttered, and then went out.

Calibration

From the theoretical models provided by the Luyteni, the engineers understood that the positively-charged EPM containment sphere would absorb electrons cast off during the tensor's compression of the sphere's internal spinning osmium ions, temporarily reversing the containment unit's ionic charge, from positive to negative.

The Department of Materials Engineering at the University of Tokyo, who constructed the depleted osmium EPM containment unit, had incorporated a magnetically shielded probe within the EPM sphere. The probe, consisting of a graphite collection surface with a permanent magnet underneath, measured the particles inside the osmium sphere's electron biteout, or its (P)Es.

Before calibration, the embedded probe was reporting positive 4.24 (P)Es, reflecting the positively-charged depleted osmium sphere's empty particle to electron biteout strength.

When the engineers on the collider floor activated the tensor assembly's controller, its processor initialized the KEK-GenQ accelerator and the tensor assembly's electromagnetic actuators. Positively-charged osmium ions began flooding the accelerator. Seconds later, the particles, now accelerated to almost the speed of light, were injected into the EPM containment unit.

The EPM containment unit, fluorescing from the tensor assembly's field interaction with the metallic osmium casing, maintained the spinning particles at near-c momentum inside the sphere.

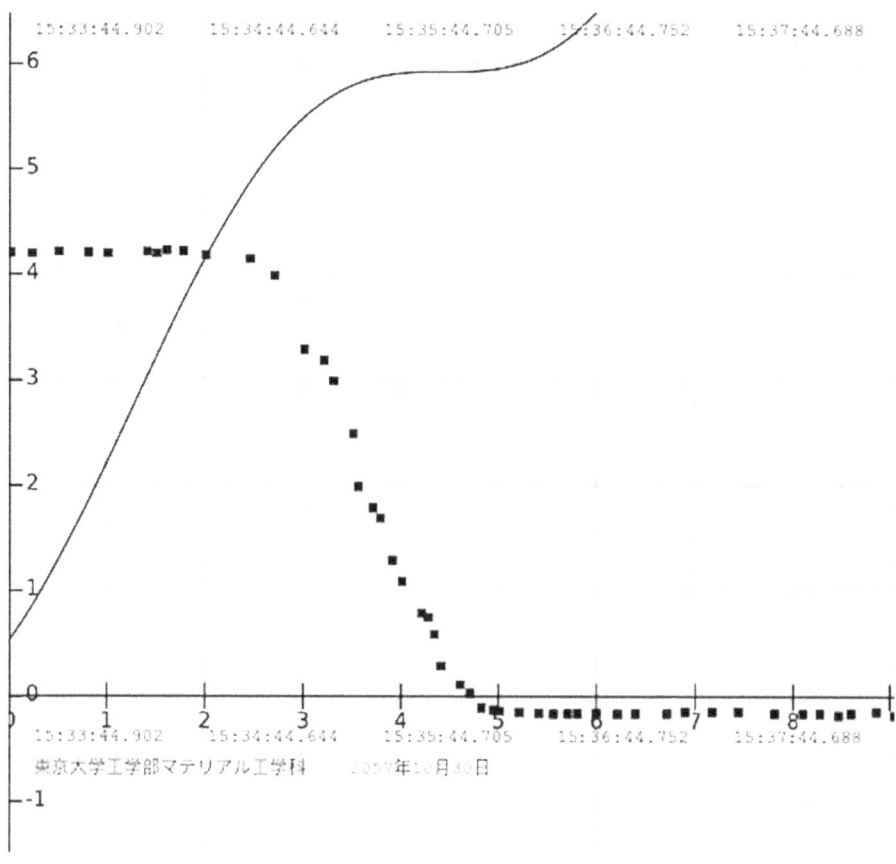

Figure 29 - University of Tokyo Department of Materials Engineering containment (P)E probe track, recording the first singularity generation on October 30, 2067.

Throughout the early morning hours of October 30, 2067, the tensor assembly's electromagnetic field began compressing the spinning osmium ions inside the sphere. By 15:30 in the afternoon, the ions began to cast off their remaining electrons, reducing the containment unit's positive ionic charge. At that moment, a gravitational field began to form on the surface of the compressed ion's nucleus, warping space-time within the sphere.

Midori Yamaguchi, Professor of high-performance electron devices at the University of Tokyo, was monitoring the EPM containment unit's embedded (P)E probe when she noticed what appeared to be a drop in the depleted osmium sphere's positive ionic charge.

Figure 30 - Mankind's first EPM singularity being calibrated on the P-SEQS collider floor, October 30, 2067. Image courtesy National Physical Laboratory Archives, London, UK.

Struggling to be heard over the deafening hum of the room's massive electrical capacitors, Yamaguchi frantically pointed to the probe's display indicator and shouted, "Charge dropping!"

At 15:35:44 on October 30, 2067, space-time itself ripped, creating a singularity inside the sphere.

News and media organizations immediately flashed the announcement around the world; reporting mankind's first stable singularity had been achieved at the P-SEQS facility.

For the next 6 hours and 14 minutes, the P-SEQS project principals watched breathless, as the fluorescing ultraviolet hole began to grow on the collider floor.

At 21:48, the singularity split into its two event horizons, bracketing the containment sphere. Minutes later, the NPL team joined those assembled on the collider floor and reported the tensor assembly's calibration cycle had successfully concluded and the singularity's two event horizons were now stabilized, maintaining at 1.3 gigawatts of power.

Spatially-dilated 10 meters apart, the event horizons were maintained for 52 minutes as a series of test objects were passed through the fluorescing ultraviolet voids, culminating in a rhesus monkey, "Yuri", named for early space astronaut Yuri Gagarin *(See: "I Saw It Drop – the Biography of Prof. Midori Yamaguchi" – by Tatsuke Yoshizawa; NAFS-Archive Unit 33, 2s - (ar) 2088, File: D49A692702)*.

First Temporal Singularity

The Earth's first temporal singularity was achieved on December 19, 2068.

Precisely following the Luyteni temporal instructions, Dr. Manfred Krieger, Director of Experimental Physics at P-SEQS, calibrated the singularity's two event horizons 10 meters apart on the collider floor.

Figure 31 - Dr. Manfred Krieger, Director of Experimental Physics at P-SEQS. Photo taken December 23, 2068, outside the P-SEQS collider building. Image courtesy Ludwig-Maximilians-Universität München, München, Konföderation der Germanischen Staate.

With the distant and near horizons stabilized, Krieger initialized the facility's tunneling regulator, releasing the tensor assembly's hold on the distant event horizon for precisely 0.142 seconds, before returning control back to the tensor.

A few seconds later, as he was preparing to step through the singularity's close event horizon, Krieger abruptly emerged from the distant event horizon.

For a moment, both Kriegers stared at each other across the EPM collider floor, before the shocked staff shouted at the "first" Krieger to proceed thru.

The distant event horizon, it was later confirmed, was 18.2 seconds "older" than the near horizon.

Krieger, mankind's first "time traveler", replicated the experiment the following week before an assembled group of scientific and government leaders, actually shaking hands with himself before transiting through the near horizon.

After answering questions for several minutes, Krieger concluded the demonstration by stepping back through the distant event horizon, to emerge once again from the near horizon.

International Temporal Treaty

On April 16, 2070, the 36 nations directly involved in the P-SEQS project signed the International Temporal Treaty (ITT).

The treaty outlined a set of standards governing all future research, development, and use of temporal singularities. The treaty obligated all temporal incursions to be authorized by a member-nation governing council, the Conseil Temporel International (CTI), or "International Temporal Council" headquartered in Geneva, Switzerland.

Under the treaty, only selected member nations were permitted to initiate limited temporal incursions subject to strict council oversight and compliance with temporal guidelines.

As of 2145, there were 7 CTI-authorized member nations; The Peoples Republic of China, the North America Federated States, the Confederation of Germanic States, Great Britain, Japan, Brazil, and India.

Non-Temporal Governance

In 2083, a group of 41 tourists purchased transit passes from Evanston Space Ventures in Florida to visit the Descartes crater in the south-central highlands of Luna. Ignoring warnings about increasing solar flare activity, the company operators permitted the group to transition to Luna wearing standard 6-hour EVA suits.

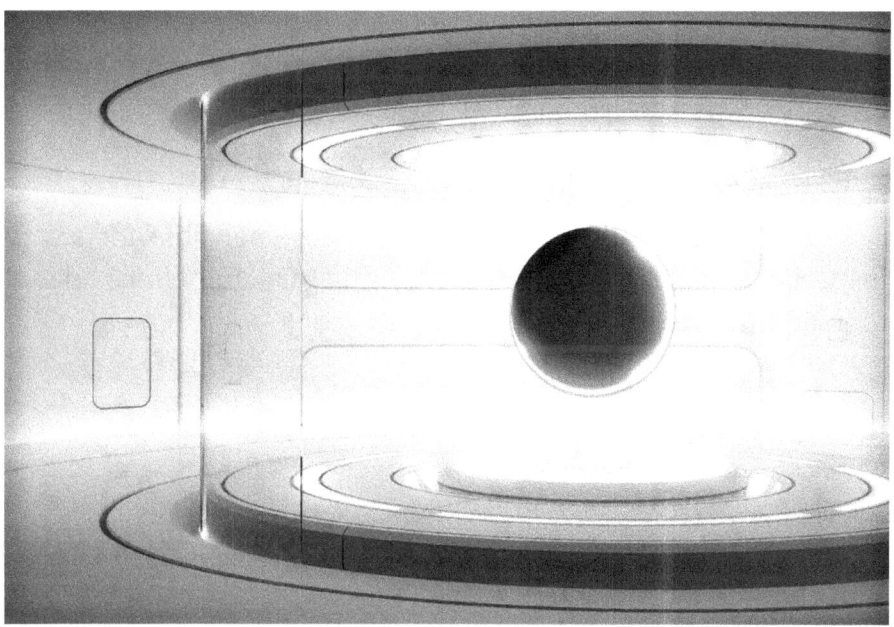

Figure 32 - A 0.74-meter EPM singularity, calibrated at -0.148 P(E) with 0.00 spatial differentiation, circa 2142. Image courtesy University of Oxford Quantum Engineering Department, Oxford, United Kingdom.

93 minutes into the trip, solar flare activity disrupted all Lunar extra-terrestrial EPM singularities. Before the flares subsided 9 hours later, all but one of the Evanston group had

suffocated; the first human deaths on the Lunar surface. The sole survivor, a 7-year old girl, only survived after her father, and then her mother disconnected their own O2 tanks and attached them to the child's EVA emergency intake line.

After the Evanston accident, the Earth's EPM-capable nations established the 2084 Autorité Internationale Singulière de la Matière Phasique Exotique (AISMPE), or the "International Exotic Phased Matter Singularity Authority".

Under AISMPE guidelines, all EPM singularity operators were required to be licensed. In addition, all extra-terrestrial settlement or commercial development was subject to approval by a (then) 21-nation committee.

In 2108, the committee was expanded to 44 members, and again in 2131 to its present 62 members.

In addition to licensing, AISMPE is responsible for safety inspections and the publication of regulatory guidelines related to non-temporal EPM use.

Singularity Usage

Stabilized exotic phased-matter singularities are widely used for travel, shipping, and on extremely rare occasions, for CTI-authorized temporal incursions. Stabilized singularities now connect virtually every corner of the Earth, the Lunar communities, the orbiting stations, and the Martian colonies.

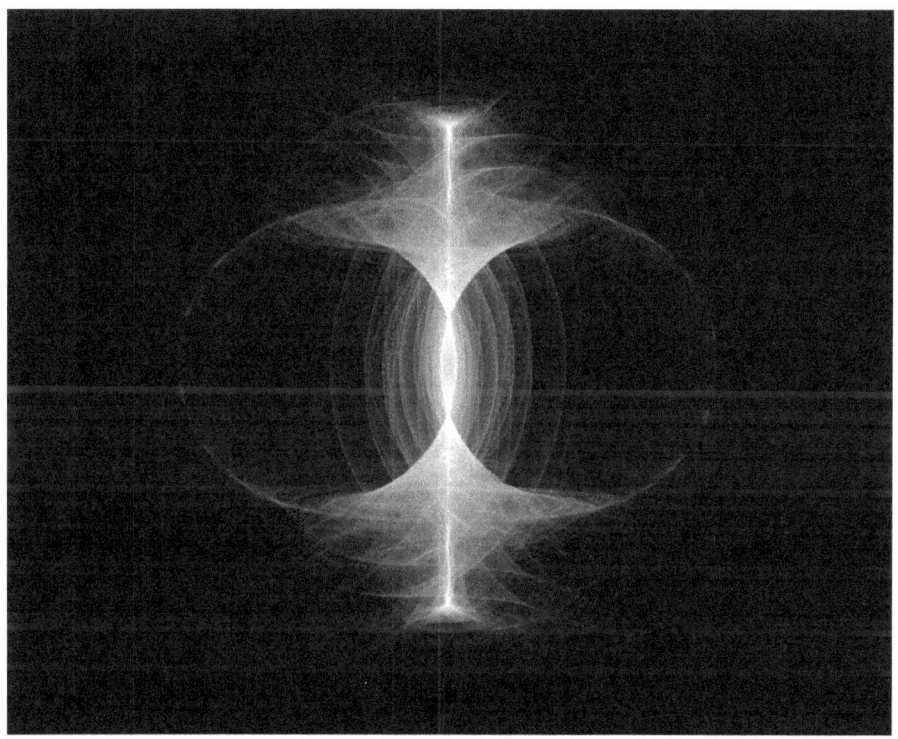

Figure 33 - PNE resonance scan of a singularity at the moment of quantum separation/coupling. Image courtesy: Istituto Nazionale di Fisica Nucleare, Rome, Italy, circa 2135.

Following the announcement of the Earth's first successful

singularity, mankind's focus shifted to reducing the EPM singularity's enormous power requirements, increasing the spatial distance between event horizons, and reducing the time required to achieve calibration. With the world transitioning from nuclear to fusion power, and from silicon to quantum-based computing, both the unit size and energy cost of EPM transit devices began to dramatically decrease.

The introduction of the EPM singularity was the primary factor contributing to the demise of the world's airline industry. Within 10 years of their introduction, self-contained EPM facilities measuring less than 10 square meters were being installed around the globe at airports and other mass-transit facilities.

By 2102, virtually all Earth-based "airports" had been repurposed as EPM transit stations. For less than the price of a former airplane ticket, a person could transit instantly to their destination city, provided the transit station had scheduled a calibration with that city.

Corporations and wealthy executives maintained private EPM facilities for business and personal travel. "Locked" EPM stations, singularities indefinitely calibrated between two fixed points, facilitated affordable daily commutes between major population centers.

Scattering particle field technologies, developed in 2108 from a Luyteni design model, provided privacy and security to those wishing to deny EPM access to their facilities.

In February 2085, the first orbital EPM platform was launched by Beijing-startup Xie-Deng. The small, 3.5-meter platform was the first EPM facility to be itself transited through another EPM facility into low-earth orbit. At the time, it was the furthest EPM device from the Earth. Marketed as an affordable satellite deployment platform, the self-contained EPM-equipped orbiting platform was the forerunner of later EPM-equipped manufacturing, scientific, commercial, and residential orbital stations.

According to data provided by the Phasenverschobene Materie Sicherheitsrat ("Phase-Shifted Matter Security Council") in Berlin, in 2148 mankind had 64,391 EPM transit stations in operation, including the Embraes Fast Transit Network between the Earth and Mars *(See: "2148 Bericht des Phasenverschobene Materie Sicherheitsrat"; NAFS-Archive Unit 87, 9h - (ar) 2148, File: DD512CFCC4).*

End Summary File: 850DC689DD//:QKDS-51676F54A

Extra-Terrestrial Colonization

Begin Summary File: A3038951DB//:QKDS-51676F54A

Schiller Mining Colony

<u>Construction</u>

The first permanent Luna colony was chartered in July 2088 by Texas, NAFS-based Schiller Mining Company. The colony was established to extract helium-3 (He-3) from the upper layer of Luna's regolith soil.

Between 2080 and 2120, helium-3 was in high demand for use in early fusion reactors. By fusing the helium with itself, the reaction had the advantage of producing no excess neutrons during power generation; one of the first truly "clean" fusion power sources.

After receiving approval from AISMPE to construct the colony, the company's senior management conducted a symbolic groundbreaking ceremony on July 24, 2088, near the lunar equator, approximately 344 km northeast of the present Grimaldi City.

Construction of the Schiller Colony was completed on June 5, 2090. The colony consisted of an underground habitat and community ring, surrounding a central processing plant. At its peak, the colony supported 3,188 miners, technicians, supervisory, and support personnel.

The helium-3 was extracted using hundreds of RMV remote mining vehicles that tunneled several meters into the regolith soil of Luna's Oceanus Procellarum region. The RMVs transported the ore to the central processing facility where it was heated to more than 600 degrees Celsius, freeing the soil-locked helium-3. The extracted helium-3 was then shipped to the Earth via the colony's three locked EPM transit stations.

The sintered regolith, now free of its helium-3, was capable of withstanding more than 206 megapascals of pressure, more than 5 times more pressure than the strongest concrete, and was used in the construction of many of the later lunar communities.

Figure 34 - Schiller Mining Colony's fusion-powered regolith furnace in operation. Circa 2105. Image courtesy Schiller Mining Company.

During its nearly 35-years of operation, the Schiller Mining Colony transported more than 84,000 tonnes of lunar helium-3 to the Earth and was the eras largest supplier of the isotope for fusion generation, cryogenics, and medical imaging. Over the same period, the colony produced more than 1.2 billion tonnes of construction-grade sintered regolith.

The history of the Schiller Colony is a history of "firsts". The first extra-terrestrial birth took place at the colony on January 9, 2094; a baby boy, "Creciente" DaCosta, born to Angelina DaCosta, an RMV maintenance technician, and Dr. Paulo DaCosta, the colony physician.

The first extra-terrestrial marriage took place on April 5, 2096, between Michael Heath, a thermal plant supervisor, and Luli Huáng, a Shenzhen Energy contractor. The marriage, officiated by the colony civil adjudicator, was performed inside the newly completed Schiller-McDermott Geodesic Arboretum, the first permanent "park" on Luna.

The Schiller Colony was also the first company to implement an electromagnetically-suspended tubed shipping system. The magnetic rail tube, placed flush against its Luna to Earth singularity event horizon, greatly decreased shipping time and served as a model for the later Mars Fast-Transit Network *(See: "The Schiller Mining Colony" – by Alberto Russo; NAFS-Archive Unit 117, 15c - (ar) 2134, File: 46FB21C551).*

Hōfu Station

<u>JAXA Project</u>

Approximately three years after the completion of the first Lunar colony, the Japan Aerospace Exploration Agency (JAXA) announced its intent to construct the first permanently inhabited orbital station.

The station would be a financial and corporate center, constructed at an earth-orbit of 189,902 kilometers, approximately halfway between the Earth and Luna, and would be the first orbital structure to employ gravity plates based on the Luyteni's 2076 gravimetric design model.

The JAXA announcement in April 2093, was received with great excitement by the world's business community. However, when the station plans were first submitted to AISMPE for review, concerns were raised about the station's almost unilateral business focus. Almost a third of the AISMPE committee's 21 members opposed the station plans on the grounds that it did not satisfy the residency requirements for a habitat-designated colony.

Unlike the Schiller Mining Colony then in operation on Luna, the JAXA orbital station was not chartered by a business entity, nor had it been submitted as a purely commercial interest. The JAXA orbiting station had been submitted for AISMPE's consideration as a "habitat colony".

Under governance rules enacted by the then 21-member AISMPE committee, habitat colonies were given preferential financing and regulatory considerations and were subject to AISMPE International Colonial Law (AICL), rather than their sponsor's corporate charter.

Ultimately, plans for the JAXA orbital station were re-designed and expanded, to satisfy the requirements for habitat-colony designation under AISMPE rules. With those revisions, one-third of the colony's surface area was zoned for purely residential habitation. Business and corporate interests were still strongly featured but would be subject to AICL jurisdiction rather than their individual corporate charters.

As part of the JAXA station's promotion, residents who purchased habitat space on the station were permitted to submit a proposed colony name for consideration. More than 190,000 applications were submitted for the 3,200 residential habitats. After the certification and selection process had been completed, the JAXA design team announced the station's name would be "Hōfu Station".

In 2128, Hōfu Station's permanent resident population was 11,232 people.

Including assignment staff transiting daily from Earth and Luna, the station typically has between 32,400 and 35,500 inhabitants.

Design Considerations

Hōfu Station was designed as four interconnected half-sphere domes, each with a surface area comprising 78.5 hectares (194 acres). The sub-surface of each quadrant houses its graviton generation panels, primary and backup fusion plants, water reclamation and sewage processing, reserve O2, He-3, and H2O, and maintenance bays holding manned and remote-operated maintenance vehicles.

Within each domed quadrant, elevated electromagnetic rail systems and walkway bridges connect the quadrant's commercial structures; primarily banking, corporate, and financial centers.

In accordance with AISMPE rules then in place, Hōfu Station's exterior was required to be constructed with a redundant atmospheric pressure seal. Should a micro-meteorite compromise the station's external seal, a secondary seal would prevent catastrophic loss of atmosphere.

Figure 35 - Quadrant 2 Fujioka Financial Center lobby, Hōfu Station, day cycle. Circa 2133. Image courtesy JAXA.

This regulatory requirement presented the station's designers with a challenge, however, as they wished to provide the colony residents with spacious views of the Earth, Luna, the stars, and the sun.

The station's engineers appealed to the Japan Chemical Industry Association. The solution they delivered was both practical and innovative; a transparent gelatinized sodium silicate solution that, when exposed to a vacuum, solidified rapidly. When sandwiched between durable hydrogen-infused polymer layers, the "gelatinized glass" was both extremely strong, transparent, and in the case of a micro-meteorite impact, self-sealing. The hydrogen-infused polymer layers also provided protection from both solar particle radiation and galactic cosmic rays.

The station's designers were so impressed with the concept, they undertook an unprecedented redesign of the entire station, forcing yet another AISMPE review. The AISMPE review committee, however, was equally impressed with the new design and fast-tracked its approval.

Instead of the original metallic double-sealed quad-dome design, with scattered dual-paned pressurized viewing ports, the entire station would now feature geodesic-framed transparent domes, providing residents with a magnificent view of the star-filled sky. Housing units were relocated to each of the quadrant's perimeters, offering unobstructed views to the station residents.

To take advantage of the new transparent dome design, the station's orbital spin was re-calculated to replicate the Earth's 24-hour day/night cycle. Spinning slowly, the station residents experience a true dawn-to-dusk solar cycle.

The station designers also incorporated a deployable pressure shroud system, as a backup to the geodesic transparent dome. In the event of a catastrophic breach, the damaged dome section is ejected as a hermetically sealed micro-fiber shroud racing along an internal track system seals the breach, preventing further loss of atmosphere. At the same time, emergency O2 is released from the quadrant's substructure, normalizing internal atmospheric pressure.

Each circular quadrant houses five separate EPM transition devices; two 5-meter EPM transit stations (lock-calibrated to Tokyo, Japan, and New York, NAFS), and three smaller 4-meter EPM transit platforms calibrated to each of the three other quadrants.

Figure 36 - Quadrant 3 ground plaza, Hōfu Station, night cycle. Circa 2133.
Image courtesy JAXA.

The Sumitomo Bank building in Quadrant 1 also maintains a private corporate 3-meter EPM transit device capable of reaching Earth.

Following AISMPE guidelines governing extra-terrestrial colonization, each of the 3,200 residential habitats, as well as all primary internal structures, are capable of being individually pressurized.

Each structure also contains a 30-hour battery-powered

emergency heating unit, 30-hours of reserve emergency O2 and its own ECRN communication transmitter *(See: "防府駅: 百万の光を持つ都市" – by 渡辺丹子; NAFS-Archive Unit 63, 5f - (ar) 2128, File: B53B04B369).*

Construction

The primary limiting factor in extraterrestrial construction is the diameter of an EPM singularity's event horizon.

Although singularities large enough for human transit are achievable within the power generation capabilities of most commercial entities, larger event horizons create exponentially greater power requirements. Beyond a certain diameter, a singularity's calibration requirements simply exceed most commercially-available power generator capabilities.

In the early days of EPM deployment, between 0.9 and 1.2 gigawatts of power was required to calibrate a 4-meter diameter singularity; well within the range of first-generation helium-3 fusion reactors.

A 5-meter diameter singularity, however, required between 44 and 62 gigawatts of power to calibrate, while a 6-meter diameter singularity required more than 580 gigawatts of power, restricting larger singularity calibration to governmental or multi-corporation consortiums.

JAXA intended to pre-fabricate the thousands of habitat units on Earth, and then transit the completed modules via an EPM singularity to Hōfu station.

At the time, the largest EPM transit station in Japan was a government-owned 7.6-meter diameter unit at the Chofu Aerospace Center Aerodrome in Mitaka-shi, Tokyo. Within 18 months, the Aerospace Center Aerodrome complex had been redesigned into a manufacturing and transition facility.

To accommodate the diameter of the Chofu EPM singularity, all habitats and other prefabricated structures were restricted to a maximum height and width of 5m x 5m. Larger structures that could not be pre-fabricated were transited in sections and assembled on-site.

Figure 37 - Hōfu Station residential module, in "sleep-mode" configuration. Circa 2133. Hōfu Station. Image courtesy JAXA.

The residential modules, while conforming to the 5m x 5m restriction, were 10-meters in length, with 2 modules being connected to form a completed habitat. Residents selected for colonization were required to pay for their habitat modules in full before taking possession, with the title being transferable only upon permission of the station's residential committee.

Construction of Hōfu Station began on March 2, 2095, with the deployment of four orbital pressurized platforms transited from the Chofu EPM site. At the time, the platforms were the largest objects ever transited through an EPM singularity. Once connected end-to-end in orbit, the platforms served as a staging platform for the initial construction crews.

With the completion of the 4 pressurized domes in 2097, the pace of construction increased dramatically. The thousands of pre-fabricated resident modules were all transited and installed in less than 8 months; an incredible feat of transition and installation coordination.

The primary business structures were transited as component sections through each dome's twin 5-meter EPM stations. Once assembled on-site, each building owner or leaseholder took physical possession but was not permitted to begin commercial operations until all station construction had been completed.

The station was officially opened on September 4, 2100. After a ceremonial greeting by the station's mayor, Haru Suzuki, the station's lights were dimmed to permit the newly arrived residents to experience the full stellar majesty outside of the transparent domes. The date is commemorated each year at the annual "Hoshi no Saiten" 星の祭典 ("Festival of the Stars").

Hōfu Garden

The station's transparent dome design also prompted the station's designers to incorporate a smaller, fifth greenhouse dome, constructed of the same self-sealing "gelatinized glass", and located centrally between the four connecting habitat domes at a latitudinal equivalent of 25°N.

Named "Hōfu Teien" 防府庭園 ("Hōfu Garden"), the park is today considered one of the most beautiful exo-parks ever constructed.

Construction of the garden addition began on October 9, 2097, and was completed on January 10, 2102

Nearly 30.5 hectares in size, Hōfu Teien boasts more than 40 different species of trees, including the only collection of extra-terrestrial prunus serrulata, or "sakura" cherry trees. The garden's climate and solar exposure are maintained synchronously with Tokyo, Japan, causing the trees to bloom in early April.

Figure 38 - Hōfu Garden carp pond, near Quadrant 2 entrance, Hōfu Station. Circa 2137. Image courtesy Hōfu Teien Kanri Jimusho.

A large pond, filled with carp, frogs, and game fish, is located near the entrance to quadrant 2 and is home to a collection of red-crowned cranes. The wing-clipped cranes are cared for by the station's Garden Conservatory Foundation in partnership with the Japan Wildlife Conservation Society.

Twenty-two private tea houses are located throughout the park's quiet bamboo and pine groves and are exclusively available to the colony residents and their guests. The garden's tea houses can be reserved through the station's garden administration office *(Contact: Hōfu Teien Kanri Jimusho, 6-12 Kokufuichiba, Futari-ku, Hōfu Station, ECRN: 2.2.6.12.46).*

Benton Station

Eric Benton

In January 2095, helium-3 billionaire Eric Benton announced plans to construct an extra-terrestrial casino and entertainment center outside of AISMPE's orbital jurisdiction.

Figure 39 - Eric Benton (left) speaking with the media following the AISMPE verdict, February 4, 2096. Image courtesy Benton Corporation archives.

Under the terms of the AISMPE charter, all extra-terrestrial settlements and commercial facilities located within 3 lunar distances from Earth were subject to AISMPE governance.

Benton, the largest individual shareholder in the Schiller Mining Company on Luna, was notorious for his criticism of the

AISMPE's 21-member committee, often chiding the committee for alleged excessive and unnecessary regulatory guidelines that he believed were negatively impacting the lunar mining colony's interests.

As announced, Benton's station would be constructed at what was then a breathtakingly distant 1,191,600 kilometers from the Earth. Notably, the station would be built 38,000 kilometers beyond the AISMPE committee's 3-lunar distance jurisdiction.

The AISMPE committee, furious with the announcement, issued a restraining order on February 9, 2095, to the world's EPM manufacturers, promising sanctions and license revocation to any that supplied Benton or his companies with EPM tensor, calibration, or control equipment.

<u>Benton et al v. AISMPE</u>

On May 12, 2095, Benton Station Holdings filed a lawsuit with the Supreme Court of the Confederation of Germanic States in Geneva, Switzerland, AISMPE's judicial authority.

At issue was the Benton Station Holdings' claim that AISMPE had no right to prevent manufacturers from supplying EPM technology to parties for use outside of AISMPE's explicit 3-lunar distance jurisdiction.

AISMPE's position was that its charter gave it jurisdiction over the EPM technology itself and that it had the right to restrict distribution of that technology to any party who refused to submit to AISMPE licensing and safety guidelines.

Arguing from a position of public safety, AISMPE's legal counsel frequently cited the Evanston accident in 2083 and other EPM-related industrial or operational accidents that had occurred since 2067.

Benton's counsel, however, pointed to explicit language in the AISMPE charter limiting its governance to 3-lunar distances from the Earth.

Concerned about AISMPE's assertions of jurisdictional and distribution control over their products, 22 of the 26 companies restrained by AISMPE filed briefs in support of Benton Station Holdings' position. They were joined by Brazilian aerospace agency, Embraes, then planning a network of transit platforms connecting Earth to Mars.

After a nearly 9-month trial, the court ruled in favor of Benton Station Holdings and its supporters. Though acknowledging it shared AISMPE's concerns regarding EPM safety, the court found the "3 lunar-distance" language within the AISMPE charter to be "unambiguous and irrefutable" *(See: "Benton et all v. AISMPE, BVerfG, NJW 2086, 3121 (1013 f.)"; NAFS-Archive Unit 304, 25d - (ar) 2096, File: C06D941AAD).*

Noting the 9-month trial length at a press conference, Benton described the court's decision as "giving birth to a new era of space colonization".

Way Station

When Benton announced his plans in 2095, the furthest distance an EPM singularity had been calibrated through open space was 822,514 kilometers; from the Schmitt Research building's EPM unit inside the Tsiolkovskiy crater on the far side of Luna.

To reach the targeted 1,191,600-kilometer distance from Earth, Benton was forced to construct an intermediary EPM platform beyond Luna's orbit.

Construction of the intermediary platform began on March 2, 2096, with a 3-meter by 3-meter container transited from the

Schilling Mining Colony to an orbital distance of 618,240 kilometers from Luna. The container was little more than a heated, pressurized, double-hull shell, with gravity plates under its substructure, a Bosch 220GW fusion reactor, and 2.4-meter EPM singularity unit squeezed inside.

Figure 40 - "Un Avant-Goût de Paris" (formerly Way Station), circa 2123. Image courtesy Région Parisienne Corporation.

As additional units were later transited and connected, exterior walls were sealed and interior walls removed, increasing the interior area.

Dubbed "Way Station", the completed orbital platform measured 110 by 86 meters and was 5 meters high. The original 2.4-meter EPM unit was replaced with two 4-meter EPM transit units, one focused on Luna, and the other on a point in space that would later become Benton Station.

Way Station orbits within the AISMPE charter's 3-lunar distance from Earth and is therefore under AISMPE jurisdiction. Upon its completion in October 2086, the station was inspected and re-inspected, but the inspectors were unable to prevent its final certification, which was reluctantly granted on November 11, 2096.

Way Station itself provided little in the way of amenities to Benton Station travelers, containing only the two EPM transit units, a ROM remote-operated medical bay, two restaurants, a financial kiosk, public lavatories, and a row of public-use ECRN communication pods.

Though small, the station maintained a permanent staff of 16 to 18 restaurant and facility workers, 2 transit operators, and 1 station manager *(See: "L'histoire de Un Avant-Goût de Paris" courtesy of Région Parisienne Corporation; NAFS-Archive Unit 221, 8f - (ar) 2119, File: 82D6A2CFB7).*

Benton Station Construction

Construction of Benton Station itself began on December 4, 2096, with the deployment of an ECRN signal marker transited from Way Station to the targeted 1,191,600-kilometer distance from Earth.

Unlike the circular geodesic domes of Hōfu Station, Benton Station was designed as an entertainment and resort center, with future expansion intended.

The initial plans called for the construction of an 11,000-square meter, geometrically-shaped 3,000-room hotel and casino complex floating in space. The structure's angular design allowed for additional structures to be attached later to the exterior while preserving its original appearance.

Benton station is constructed of traditional dual-paneled pressure-stabilized walls layered with hydrogenated boron nitride nanotubes to shield from particle and cosmic radiation. The walls are filled with L-5 composite metal foam, providing protection against micro-meteorite penetration.

Figure 41 - Benton Station grand concourse – Benton Station Holdings
promotional image, circa 2101. Image courtesy Benton Corporation archives.

All Benton Station rooms, including its casino floors, are capable of being immediately sealed in the event of an atmospheric breach and are equipped with pressurized puncture extinguishers within emergency panels next to every door. In addition, each sealable compartment is equipped with a 30-hour battery-powered heating unit, 30 hours of reserve emergency O2, and an ECRN communication panel linked with the station's primary ECRN communications array.

As with Hōfu Station, Benton Station is equipped with graviton generation panels, primary and backup fusion plants, water reclamation and sewage processing, reserve O2, He-3, and H2O, and maintenance bays holding remote-operated maintenance vehicles.

Construction of the primary hotel and casino facility was completed on January 18, 2101.

Figure 42 - Benton Station corridor - Benton Station Holdings promotional image, circa 2101. Image courtesy Benton Corporation archives.

To commission the facility, Eric Benton smashed a bottle of rare 1931 Hennessy cognac against the station's primary EPM transit platform's railing and then provided every attendee with free casino markers.

Expansion

From 2101 until 2108, Benton Station experienced tremendous growth. Driven by private corporate investment, the station's size quadrupled to include three additional casinos, two additional hotels, 11 restaurants, and more than 1,800 luxury suites.Benton Station hosted the first extra-terrestrial concert on February 2101, featuring singers Alexis Lopez and Lainey Cavanaugh, with magician Michael Abalos. More than 3,400 concert markers were sold, selling out the main casino showroom in less than 20 minutes.

Figure 43 - Singer Lainey Cavanaugh, performing at Benton Station, February 9, 2101. Image courtesy The Cavanaugh Experience.

The addition of a positional-stabilized external racing track in 2104 provided guests with the ability to wager on high-speed zero-gravity remote controlled racing from the safety of the pressurized station's viewing boxes.

At its height, Benton Station served more than 18,200 guests each day, and maintained a permanent staff of 1,035 *(See: "The History of Benton Station" by Aldo Capella; NAFS-Archive Unit 19,*

226k - (ar) 2122, File: 4E380A0188).

2108 Calabrese Murder

On May 1, 2108, Benton Station manager Lorenzo Russo was arrested at Way Station by the Luna Colonial Marshal's office on a charge of murder.

Though illegal under AISMPE International Colonial Law at that time, prostitution was common on Benton Station as the station was located outside of AISMPE's legal jurisdiction.

On April 14, 2108, the casino's security cameras recorded station manager Lorenzo Russo leaving the casino floor with Nicole "Nikki" Calabrese, a 22-year old prostitute from the Copernicus colony on Luna (now Copernicus City). When Calabrese later failed to return to Luna, her family filed a missing person's report.

The Luna Colonial Marshal's office traced Calabrese through transit station logs to Way Station and then to Benton Station where she was known to work, but found no record of any return transit.

Lacking jurisdiction inside Benton Station itself, the Colonial Marshal's office was forced to appeal to the station's security manager's office for assistance, however, their requests were ignored or hampered by Russo himself.

Finally, threatened with a public scandal, and after reviewing the security camera recordings showing Russo leaving the casino with Calabrese, Benton Station Holdings executives ordered the station's security office to detain Russo and transport him to Way Station, where marshals took him into custody.

Calabrese's body was never found and was believed to have been concealed within a sol-bound waste shipment.

Russo was convicted of murder under AISMPE International Colonial Law and sentenced to life internment on Earth. Russo, however, appealed the conviction to the appellate court in Geneva on the grounds that Benton Station was outside of AISMPE's jurisdiction.

The appellate court reluctantly agreed, and overturned the conviction, explaining that, while Russo had been arrested at Way Station, the crime itself had occurred outside of AISMPE's 3-lunar distance jurisdiction *(See: "Justice Denied: the Nikki Calabrese Story" by Aldo Capella; NAFS-Archive Unit 196, 22w - (ar) 2124, File: 15103AF750).*

Russo's release caused many within Earth's colonial advocacy community to reconsider for the first time the wisdom of the AISMPE 3-lunar distance jurisdictional limit.

Originally intended to promote colonial expansion, the 3-lunar distance rule was now seen as contributing to a lawless "wild west" atmosphere where criminals could operate with impunity.

On November 2, 2108, after months of hearings on the matter, and despite fierce opposition by the Benton Corporation, the AISMPE governing committee dropped the 3-lunar distance rule from its charter, replacing it with a new rule placing "all extra-terrestrial human habitations or enterprises" under AISMPE jurisdictional control. The new AISMPE charter was then signed by a new 44-member nation committee.

Bankruptcy and Abandonment

Following the announcement in 2108 that Benton Station would now be under AISMPE jurisdictional control, Benton Station Holdings investors began selling off their interests in the property. Share prices plummeted. Public outrage over Russo's release also fueled angry demonstrations against the holding company's parent, Benton Corporation.

On March 2, 2109, Benton Station suspended operations and Benton Station Holdings filed for relief under the Confederation of Germanic States insolvency laws.

On March 11, 2109, Eric Benton held a press conference, announcing his resignation from the holding company's board and his intent to sell or otherwise liquidate the station. Benton never completed the station's sale or liquidation, however, suffering a stroke and dying on October 3, 2109, at the age of 62. Benton Station Holdings was then placed in a trust by the court.

By 2110, Benton Station was, for all practical intent, abandoned. Over the next several years, much of its furnishings and internal components were stolen by Luna transit thieves before a quantum scattering field was installed in 2116.

Current Status

By 2119, with improvements in EPM calibration placing Benton Station within direct transit range of Earth and Luna, Way Station was no longer needed as an intermediary transit platform.

In 2122, Way Station was sold to the Région Parisienne Corporation, who renamed the small station "Un Avant-Goût de Paris" and converted the station's two small restaurants into a single restaurant specializing in French cuisine.

In 2128, Benton Station itself was sold to a group of southeast-Asian businessmen. The grand concourse and main casinos were converted into commercial districts, while those luxury suites still capable of pressurization were converted into private residences and sold to residents. The hotels were gutted for their furnishings, and then converted into low cost rental habitats.

Benton Station's resident population in 2140 was estimated to be approximately 6,200 people, however, no official census has been taken since 2128.

The station residents answer to a governing council, who manage all internal station affairs. The council levies a "station tax" on all residents and visitors, ostensibly to maintain the station's systems.

Figure 44 - Benton Station grand concourse, circa 2140. Image courtesy AISMPE Colonial Archives, File B-6044.

While officially still under AISMPE jurisdiction and subject to International Colonial Law, Benton Station today is widely known for crime, gambling, vice, and other illicit activities *(See: "2140 AISMPE Transit Advisory" – pg 13; NAFS-Archive Unit 74, 18c - (ar) 2140, File: 951C5DE0A9).*

Mars Fast-Transit Network

Embraes

With the launch of the first orbital EPM platform by Beijing-startup Xie-Deng in 2085, the dream of colonizing Mars moved beyond the realm of wishful planning into reality.

In January 2090, the Brazilian government's newly-formed Empresa Brasileira de Aeroespacial S.A. (Embraes) approached the NAFS' National Aeronautics and Space Administration (NASA) with a proposal to jointly construct man's first colony on Mars.

By agreement of the parties, Embraes would construct and maintain a network of transit stations in orbit between the Earth and Mars, while NASA would facilitate construction of the colony itself.

Despite Brazilian government-backing, Embraes was a relative newcomer in the field of orbital transit platform development and was forced to solicit outside proposals for the actual network design.

In May 2090, Embraes received an unexpected proposal from the Central Japan Railway (JR Tokai) to assist with the development of the network. After considering the Japanese company's more than 90-year history developing mass transit, automated transportation systems, and its engineering experience with maglev rail systems, Embraes accepted the proposal.

To accommodate Embraes' contract terms with NASA, JR Tokai engineers were required to work through the Embraes offices in São Paulo, Brazil, and all designs were required to be approved by the Brazilian government's Ministério dos

Transportes, or "Ministry of Transportation".

Network Design

At the time the project was announced, the furthest distance an EPM singularity had been calibrated through open space was approximately 822,000 kilometers.

During the periods of time when the planet's orbital separation would be at its minimum, at 54.6 million kilometers, at least 66 EPM transit stations would be required to connect the two planets.

However, during the planet's maximum orbital separation period, at 401 million kilometers, more than 487 transit platforms would have been needed to connect the planets, ignoring the fact that such a straight-line transit would have also taken passengers through the sun.

As a result, the network planners realized they would not be able to provide year-round transit between Earth and Mars. Instead, they opted for a seasonal transit model, permitting transit at only certain times of the year, when the orbits of the two planets reduced the number of required EPM transitions.

Building from this design model, the designers calculated 3,960 EPM transit platforms would be needed to provide a 48-million-kilometer wide network of orbital stations between the two planets, guaranteeing at least 2.5 months of uninterrupted transition capability.

Before deployment actually began in 2094, however, advances in EPM field strength had increased the calibrated distance between two singularity horizons to more than 1.6 million kilometers, reducing the number of stations required to 2,040, while increasing the breadth of the network to more than 96-million-kilometers, and the corresponding transit "season" to more than 5 months.

Once deployed, a traveler might transit between 40 and 90 transitions during periods of minimal orbital separation. During periods of maximum orbital separation, a traveler might transit "diagonally" between 1800 or more EPM platforms.

To accommodate emergency or mechanical failure situations, the platforms would be placed in orbit so as to keep a transiting capsule within range of at least two platforms ahead at any time.

Though more expensive than a lunar or near-earth orbital transition, an "in-season" Earth to Mars transition can generally be completed in less than an hour *(See: "Mars Fast Transit Network: An Engineering Marvel" – by H. R. Thompson; NAFS-Archive Unit 224, 10g - (ar) 2107, File: 4EF570B35A).*

Transit Capsule Design

Due to the zero-gravity environment inside the FTN platforms, the system designers quickly realized that a magnetic levitation (maglev) system would be the only viable transit method. Any other method of transiting the network would be a slow and costly proposition.

Within a self-contained, magnetically-levitated capsule, passengers would be able to transit between the two planets in one to two hours. As a result, no food services would be required, and only minimal lavatory accommodations would be necessary.

By contrast, a slower-moving transport would significantly increase the transit time, forcing the network's operators to provide food services, first aid, and security accommodations in accordance with AISMPE extraterrestrial travel guidelines.

Considerable discussion was held regarding whether or not

to equip the transit capsules with gravity plating. Initially, the project's budgetary committee would not approve the costly addition, however, after reviewing zero-gravity transport videos of airsick passengers, the committee capitulated and approved the installation of gravity plates for the transiting capsules.

Figure 45 - Embraes Earth-to-Mars FTN (Fast Transit Network) passenger capsule, circa 2133. Image courtesy Empresa Brasileira de Aeroespacial S.A.

As originally designed, each transit capsule would be approximately 18 meters long and would be capable of carrying up to 60 passengers or the equivalent space in cargo.

The capsules themselves would be pressurized, gravity-equipped, and capable of supplying 90-hours of emergency O2 and heat in the event of a network outage. Each capsule would also be equipped with an emergency ECRN transmitter, linked to the main transit network.

Platform Design

The orbital platforms were designed as 100-meter long, pressurized tubes with 5-meter EPM transit singularity platforms at either end.

Fusion-powered ion thrusters would maintain the platform's orbital position in relation to the network.

Figure 46 - Embraes Earth-to-Mars FTN (Fast Transit Network) station, São Paulo, Brazil, circa 2133. Image courtesy Empresa Brasileira de Aeroespacial S.A.

Given the zero-gravity environment, the system designers needed to ensure a transiting capsule would remain oriented to align with the maglev rail system as it transited the network. Unlike similar systems on the earth, gravity would not keep the capsule on the rails. To meet this requirement, the maglev rail was designed as a T-bar, with the capsule gripping the upper crossed rail as it transited the network. Even if interrupted mid-transit, the capsule would be held securely by the rail.

The control processor for every EPM unit synchronizes the orientation of both event horizons to maintain their alignment. JR Tokai engineers, therefore, needed only to introduce a capture device into the maglev rail system, to ensure the capsule seamlessly slid into the platform's T-rail upon entry into the platform. The T-rail design, in combination with the EPM controller's orientation synchronization, would keep the capsule locked within each platform and guarantee a smooth transit.

Unlike the fast maglev rail systems on the Earth, the FTN maglev system is designed to operate at much slower speeds. Typically, capsules transit each 100-meter platform in 8 seconds, approximately 1/7th the speed of the Earth's maglev systems. The reduced speed allows the platform to engage its emergency braking system, if necessary, without causing injury to the capsule's passengers.

In the event of a platform failure ahead of a transiting capsule, the departing platform's quantum-controlled processors would automatically re-calibrate the outgoing EPM singularity to the nearest alternate platform. In the unlikely event that no EPM platform was within range, the capsule would be "captured" by the platform's internal braking system and held in place inside the platform, pending a decision from the controller to either return the capsule to its point of origin, or re-route the capsule to another platform in the network.

Since the orbiting platforms were not intended for passenger occupation, the platform's themselves would not be equipped with gravity plating. To accommodate unforeseen emergency situations, however, each orbiting platform would be deployed with sufficient emergency food, water, and oxygen to support 60 people for 30 days. Each platform would also have an ECRN emergency beacon, and an emergency power hookup, to permit a stranded capsule to maintain its internal gravity and heating from the orbiting platform's fusion reactors.

Two Blosch "Series J" 65-gigawatt fusion reactors would power the platform's EPM units as well as the magnetic levitation system between the units.

Given the spatial distance between the orbiting platforms, calibrating a singularity to the next platform typically requires between 2.6 and 6.3 gigawatts of power. Maintaining a calibrated singularity requires between 122 and 585 megawatts of power. The maglev rail system between the two EPM units, and the emergency braking system requires 4 megawatts of power. Finally, the orbit-stabilizing ion thrusters consume 8 megawatts of power while in use.

Although a smaller "Series G" reactor would have supplied all of the platform's power requirements, the network engineers pressed for the more-powerful Series J reactors, to accommodate the possible later addition of gravity plating to the platform, should such an enhancement be deemed necessary for maintenance reasons. The larger reactors would also ensure uninterrupted emergency power for any captured capsule. Finally, it was expected that advances in EPM calibration would continue to increase the range between two event horizons, and the network designers wished to have enough power available to accommodate that anticipated future need.

The platforms themselves would be constructed of dual pressure-stabilized walls layered with hydrogenated boron nitride nanotubes to shield from particle and cosmic radiation, and filled with L-5 composite metal foam, providing protection from micro-meteorite penetration.

Construction

Construction of the network began on January 18, 2092, with the dedication of a 610-hectare manufacturing center north of the Reservatorio Paulo de Paiva Castro water reservoir in São Paulo, Brazil.

One of the first facilities constructed was the "shipyard" complex, a 1.5-hectare transition station with four 5-meter diameter EPM transit platforms linked by a rail system to the rest of the center. Each EPM platform was powered by a separate Eletrobrás 70-gigawatt fusion power plant.

Construction of the various manufacturing buildings took more than 2 years and involved companies from more than 34 nations.

Blosch Fusion constructed an entire manufacturing and assembly facility on the site in order to produce the more than 4,000 Series J fusion reactors anticipated for the project.

Helium-3 for the reactors was secured under a 25-year contract with the Schiller Mining Company's facility on Luna.

Japanese exotic metals manufacturer Shinko-Fujita secured the hull contract after completing its merger, and, like Blosch, constructed a large manufacturing facility on site.

JR Tokai's Railway Technical Research Institute supplied the maglev rail systems, though they were not produced on-site, but transited from the company's new manufacturing center in Nagoya, Japan.

The orbital platforms were constructed in four long sections so as to be transitable through the network's 5-meter singularities. All internal components, including the fusion reactors, the EPM components, the emergency air, water, and helium-3 fuel, were pre-installed within their respective sections. The intent was for the four quartered sections to be transited to their ultimate orbital position, where EVA-equipped engineers would seal the four sections together, assemble the EPM transit units and the maglev tube, and connect the internal power and control processors.

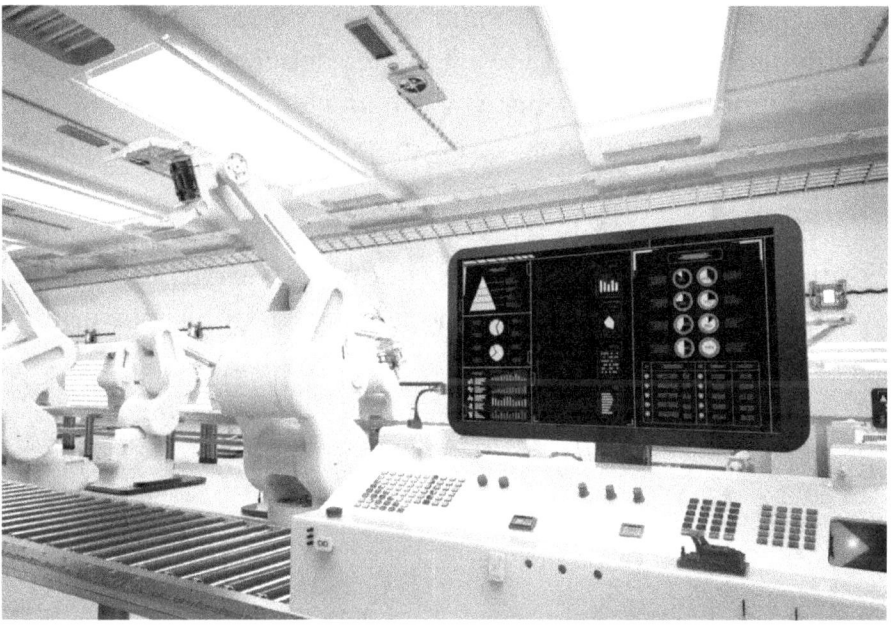

Figure 47 - Blosch Fusion assembly plant, São Paulo, Brazil, circa 2092. Image courtesy Blosch Fusion.

On June 28, 2094, at precisely 06:49 am, amid great fanfare coinciding with a total lunar eclipse over much of Brazil, the first orbital platform components were transited to a position 1.4 million kilometers from the Earth.

Assembly of that first platform took 32 hours, far beyond

the projected goal of 15 hours. By August 2094 however, with the EVA engineering teams gaining experience with the components, the assembly time per platform had been reduced to an average of 17.3 hours.

To maximize available service time for the network, the orbital platforms were deployed to fixed orbital positions relative to the Earth, not to Mars. Thus, during those periods of time when Mars was out-of-position with the network, Embraes technicians on the Earth would still be permitted to perform maintenance and upgrades to the network. As a result, construction of the network was unaffected by Mars' orbit and continued, uninterrupted, 24 hours-per-day, for the next 1,487 days.

On Thursday, July 24, 2098, the network was completed. For the next 8 months, Embraes conducted various tests on the system, including simulated emergency re-routing, power loss, and meteor damage testing.

Arch-Gale Colony

<u>Preparations</u>

With the completion of the Mars Fast Transit Network (FTN) on July 24, 2098, the North America Federated States' National Aeronautical Space Agency (NASA) commenced preparations to deploy its primary engineering and construction teams to Mars.

NASA had been preparing for this effort for more than 8 years. More than 115,000 engineers, scientists, technicians, and support personnel from more than 70 nations had been directly involved in the effort, making it the largest and costliest project man had ever undertaken, surpassing even the P-SEQS project in Europe.

The date set to begin the deployment process was June 6, 2099, when Mars' orbit brought the planet to within 1 astronomical unit (AU) of the earth, or 149,568,414 kilometers; within range of the new FTN.

To facilitate the deployment effort, 180 specialized transit capsules had been constructed to ship the hundreds of pieces of disassembled heavy equipment and the thousands of cargo containers through the newly-completed fast transit network. The special capsules also facilitated rotation of the construction crews between the two planets.

More than 1,500 construction engineers had trained for more than 5 years under simulated Martian terrain conditions in the deserts of Utah to construct the primary habitat dome in less than three months. The dome, constructed from concreted regolith soil, would be nearly 0.8 hectares in diameter and partially-buried below the surface. The structure would house the initial colony's 852 inhabitants, manufacturing and tooling facilities, 10 colonial medical bays, and a nearly 0.25-hectare greenhouse.

To supplement the construction crews and provide the colony residents with additional labor, Luxembourg-based FANUC Automation S.A. designed an SDU self-directed unit specifically for operation in Mar's cold, thin atmosphere. Built on the company's reliable Series 4 SDU platform, 260 of these Series 4(M) SDUs would accompany the construction crews to Mars and then remain behind to support the colonists.

Figure 48 - FANUC Series-4(M) SDUs under construction in Luxembourg, 2097. Image courtesy FANUC Automation S.A.

While construction of the primary habitat was underway, more than 700 secondary engineers would begin assembling the site's four Blosch Series-K 110 gigawatt fusion reactor plants, its external manufacturing and auxiliary buildings, and the CO_2 solid oxide electrolysis plants needed to extract oxygen from the Martian atmosphere *(See: "Mars Gale Colony Preliminary Equipment and Personnel Estimate - NASA Colonial Records (Released)"; NAFS-Archive Unit 414, 83h - (ar) 2094, File: 74F5807BF7).*

Water

NASA's designers understood water to be the colony's least replenishable resource, so every effort was taken to maximize water conservation. The sealed dome habitat would be equipped with internal atmospheric condensers, to reclaim water vapor and maintain optimum humidity inside the structure.

The colony's human and animal waste would be processed through a separate water reclamation facility.

Finally, a distillation plant would be constructed proximal to the habitat structure to distill water from the frozen sub-surface ice of the planet.

Water on Mars exists primarily as ice below the surface. In many places, the ice sheet can be found only one to two meters beneath the surface, and in some places, measures to a depth of more than 100 meters.

To supply the colony with water, NASA engineers developed a self-directing sub-surface ice extraction machine, capable of crushing, compacting, and depositing more than 90 tonnes of frozen ice on the Martian surface every hour.

Four of these "ice moles" were dissembled, transited to the colony site, and then reassembled by the secondary engineering teams. Once placed in operation, the machines would burrow into the Martian soil and begin pulverizing the sub-surface ice as they pushed slowly forward. The loose frozen material would be gathered and compacted inside the machine. Once filled, the machine would rise to the surface and disgorge a compacted 30-tonne ice block for later retrieval.

Figure 49 - Footprint of NASA microwave radiometer technician Tania Pavlichenko, the first human to step on Mars, June 6, 2099. Image courtesy NASA.

After being transported to the colony's distillation plant by automated sleds, the frozen blocks would be crushed, liquefied using microwaves, and their water extracted using an advanced reverse osmosis distillation process. One-atom-thick carbon membranes would be used to eliminate the perchlorates while the waste rock would then be transported by conveyor to a remote storage yard.

With all of its hydro systems in operation, the colony would be capable of recycling almost 99.92% of its water, with the balance replenished by the external atmospheric condensers or, when necessary, the ice moles. At that rate, the colony would be expected to be able to survive almost indefinitely on just the sub-surface ice in its immediate region. Should the need later arise, however, the ice-moles could be transported to more remote ice-rich regions.

Site Survey

The initial NASA survey team transited to Mars on June 6, 2099. The 14-person team transited across 1,682 FTN platforms in 3.73 hours, at an average rate of 8 seconds per transition. A "chaser" capsule followed 20-minutes behind the survey team and was captured and suspended within the final platform, to facilitate the team's later return to the Earth.

The team was transited through the final FTN platform's singularity to a location calibrated on the surface of Mars, inside the Gale Crater near Mount Sharp, in the northwestern part of the Mars Aeolis quadrangle at 5.4°S, 137.8°E.

The team disembarked from the capsule according to lots chosen before transiting. At 10:46:12 on June 6, 2099, Ukrainian-born NASA microwave radiometer technician Tania Pavlichenko became the first human being to step onto Mars. When Pavlichenko's name was announced, Ukrainians erupted in celebration, and the Ukrainian government immediately declared a national holiday in her honor.

The survey team's capsule was equipped with a mechanical drive system and inflatable wheels deployed from the side of the capsule. Once deployed and inflated by compressed CO_2

canisters, the wheels oriented the capsule and provided limited transport capabilities to the survey team. The capsule was also equipped with a small-cycle fusion reactor and an emergency EPM transit device capable of reaching the closest FTN platform.

Figure 50 - Mars Gale Colony Site "A" survey image, June 6, 2099. Mount Sharp in distance. Image courtesy NASA.

The survey team's mission was to identify optimum debarkation points for 60 portable, pressurized inflatable structures that would serve as staging areas for the initial construction crews, select the primary habitat location from 4 previously identified sites, collect atmospheric and soil samples, and measure the depth of the sub-surface ice within the crater.

The survey team completed its mission without incident and transited back to the FTN platform on June 7, 2099, at 04:30:53 hours. After signing their names to one of the FTN platform's interior hull plates, the team transited via the chase capsule back to Earth.

EPM Cargo Platforms & AISMPE Ceremony

The first of the construction and engineering crews were transited on June 9, 2099. The crews would have until January 15, 2100 to complete the construction of the initial habitat structure, assemble the heavy equipment units, power plants, and external facilities, and deploy the tonnes of supplies necessary to maintain the colonists for 19 months, until the next <1 AU network alignment would occur on August 30, 2101.

The first facilities to be transited were four EPM platforms and their corresponding maglev braking systems. Once assembled, the four nearest FTN orbital platforms were re-calibrated and locked to the surface platforms. Reinforced cargo ramps were transited next and connected to the end of the platforms, followed by four counter-balanced cranes to assist with removing the heavier cargo and material.

On June 14, 2099, with the four EPM platforms now assembled and their singularities locked with their orbiting platforms, the cargo capsules containing the construction and engineering crews began to arrive.

In accordance with AISMPE guidelines, no nation could claim sovereignty over any part of Mars. The 2098 revised AISMPE charter, signed by 44-member nations, specifically identified Mars as being subject to AISMPE International Colonial Law (AICL).

Within this first group was NASA Site Superintendent Francis "Frank" Kranz, and Embraes Colonial Governor Aberto Almeida. Following precise legal guidelines established by the AISMPE committee, Almeida instructed all personnel to remove themselves from the Martian surface soil. Once the crews had re-assembled on the four transit platforms, Almeida read aloud the future colony's charter as approved by the AISMPE committee. Then, at precisely 06:01:00 on June 14, 2099 (Earth local time), Almeida stepped onto the surface and planted the colony's flag.

Figure 51 - Survey Team Leader Sterling Smith (left) assisting geological technician Suzanne Reyes (right) with soil sample collection. Mars Gale Colony Site Survey, June 6, 2099. Image courtesy NASA.

From that moment, the Gale Colony was under AISMPE

legal jurisdiction, and NASA Site Superintendent Kranz assumed operational control of the construction effort.

<u>"Marscrete"</u>

Martian soil is rich in nanoparticle iron oxide. When subjected to pressure, the iron particles act as a bonding agent with the irregular-shaped regolith soil, locking the microscopic crystals together, resulting in a form of concrete many times stronger than that typically used on the Earth.

To create Mars' primary habitat dome and its supporting structures, surface soil was first passed slowly through long banks of drying ovens, subjecting the material to temperatures of 110°C for 14 hrs.

Once exiting the ovens, the soil was then mechanically sifted and separated into large hoppers according to their respective micrometer sizes (80μm, 55 μm, 40 μm, 30 μm, and 20 μm), with the larger and smaller particles discarded.

Finally, conveyors moved the aggregate material slowly through a multi-level Vale H-4 Fusion-powered furnace, subjecting it to an extreme heat (610°C) for 9 hours. This final process reduced the water content to <5% and removed nearly all of the carbon from the material.

Once cooled, the aggregate was mixed and deposited into large steel forms. Powerful impact compression units then compressed the material under great pressure at a rate of 8 mm per minute. The slow, incredibly powerful compression, forced the irregular aggregate crystals to interlock, crush-fill any voids, and bond with the iron oxide.

The resulting material, nicknamed "marscrete" by the assembly crews, had a strength of 54 MPa; more than 5 times stronger than traditional steel-reinforced concrete.

Construction

For the next 6 Earth months, NASA Site Superintendent Kranz directed one of the most complex and coordinated construction efforts in the history of mankind. The world watched in amazement as thousands of men, women, and SDUs, working through the Martian day and night, began to construct mankind's first settlement on the Red Planet.

Following a precise shipping schedule, personnel and cargo containers began to arrive. As soon as each capsule was unloaded, it was transited back through the FTM network to Earth.

Among the first items to arrive were the 60 portable, pressurized inflatable structures. The structures were maintained by dedicated teams of personnel responsible for maintaining the structure's heat and oxygen levels via portable small-cycle fusion reactors and hundreds of liquid oxygen tanks transited daily from Earth. The temporary structures would serve as temporary housing, medical facilities, and fabrication areas for the initial construction crews.

While the 60 pressurized structures were being assembled, crews of mechanical engineers began assembling the assorted earth moving equipment, including 20 RCD remote controlled dozers.

From the initial site survey, NASA project planners had selected site "A" as the optimum site for the primary habitat building. Located nearly midway between Bradbury Landing and Mount Sharp inside the Gale Crater, the survey team had determined the site to have the least amount of sub-surface ice to be removed; between 10 to 15 meters, as well as the best soil to support the habitat construction.

Once the RCDs were re-assembled, their operators relocated to one of the pressurized "huts" and began directing the dozers to begin removing the surface soil from site A.

For the next 14 days, the RCDs scraped the regolith soil from the Martian surface. Once the frozen ice sheet was uncovered approximately 4 meters beneath the surface, demolition crews arrived to drill and plant explosives to shatter the permafrost layer.

Figure 52 - Arch-Gale Colony Level 3 Warehouse Storage, circa 2108. Image courtesy AISMPE Colonial Archives, File 122013.

After removing the fractured ice, the RCDs moved back in, until a 0.8-hectare circle at a depth of 20 meters below the surface had been reached.

By July 16, the primary habitat dome's foundation had been poured and compacted, the dome's frame was in place, and the supporting atmospheric and distillation plants were under construction.

By August 23, the habitat dome was completely encased in its marscrete shell and the distillation plant was completed. A 20-man distillation crew now arrived from Earth and began processing the shattered sub-surface ice through the plant. Once purified and sealed in expandable polymer containers, the water, now slowly freezing again, was stacked nearby for later storage inside the habitat.

Figure 53 - Arch-Gale Colony Level 5 Resident Quarters, circa 2100. Image courtesy NASA.

Once the primary habitat dome had been completed, crews labored to seal the interior of the structure with a gas-impermeable liquid polymer. Though incredibly strong, tests had determined that thinner layers of the marscrete material would permit nitrogen and other gases to permeate it's interlocked crystalline structure. While no appreciable gas leakage could be detected through the habitat's much-thicker shell, colony planners felt the addition of a gas-impermeable polymer layer would be prudent, as well as prevent internal condensation from compromising the marscrete.

By September 10, the internal sealing process had been completed and the exterior of the recessed dome was backfilled and compacted against its raised lattice frame. Once completed, the dome exterior was completely homogeneous, resembling the top of a smooth red sphere rising from the rough surface of the planet.

By September 13, Four of the six CO_2 solid oxide electrolysis plants had been completed, and two of the four Blosch Series K fusion reactors were brought online. Once the electrolysis plants were under power, the dome was pressurized. After assorted safety and pressure checks, the construction crews moved out of the inflatable huts and into the much larger structure.

The 18 manufacturing and auxiliary buildings and the 6 CO_2 solid oxide electrolysis plants were completed by December 4. Two days later, the remaining two Blosch fusion reactors came online and two of the portable EPM platforms were relocated inside the habitat dome and re-calibrated.

Greenhouse controversy

One of the more controversial issues the colony planners had to address was whether to introduce earth organisms into the Martian environment.

While the domed habitat structure would be hermetically sealed, the fact remained that human and animal waste contains viruses, germs, bacteria, and parasitic organisms not found on Mars. The planners realized that no matter what steps might be taken to sterilize or contain such waste, Earth organisms would eventually be introduced into the Martian environment.

Figure 54 - Arch-Gale Colony Facilities Operation Center, circa 2100. Image courtesy NASA.

Accordingly, the colony's designers determined it would be counter-productive to attempt to prevent such contamination. Instead, the designers embraced the inevitability of Earth organisms being transplanted on Mars. Accordingly, the 0.25-hectare greenhouse inside the habitat dome was designed to use a mixture of 125 tonnes of bacteria-rich organic composted bio-matter shipped from the Earth, to be mixed with the Martian soil and fertilized with dehydrated waste from the colony's waste reclamation plant.

The greenhouse proposition was met with violent rejection by environmental activists, however, determined to preserve the 'purity' of the Martian environment.

Ultimately, once the activists were forced to acknowledge that, only by abandoning any plans to colonize Mars altogether could its native environment be preserved, they capitulated.

Primary habitat

With all primary structures now in operation, the focus shifted to completing the primary habitat's internal facilities. The initial construction crews and the secondary engineers now transited back to earth and were replaced by hundreds of experienced orbital station craftsmen and engineers.

Although the habitat structure was constructed on a planetary surface, the habitat's internal facilities mirrored that of an orbital station. Each of the more than 1,000 colonist quarters would be fitted with pressurized doors, emergency heat and reserve O2, and an ECRN communication panel. The room's occupant would be allowed to communicate with other colony residents or tie into the ECRN communication network through a dish placed on top of nearby Mount Sharp.

The primary habitat itself was constructed as five basic levels.

The lowest and largest level, level 5, was designated for colonist quarters.

The fourth level contained the colony's cafeteria, six of the ten medical bays, several recreation and communal gathering places, and also formed the ground floor of the internal greenhouse, which extended upward into the third level.

The third level, at ground level with the surface of the planet, was reserved for tooling, manufacturing, research, warehouse storage, waste processing, facility management, atmospheric condensers, the remaining four medical bays, water and power distribution, and the upper half of the greenhouse.

The second level was designated for the facilities operation center, communications, and security.

The top, or first level, was designated for the colony's administrative offices.

Construction of the primary habitat was completed on December 28, 2099.

The Colonists

Unlike the residents of Hōfu Station or the Lunar colonies, the 852 founding colonists selected for the Gale Colony were all professional technicians or engineers. Most of the colonists were between the ages of 35 and 50. 64 of the colonists were married couples. 3 were single parents. Only 23 children accompanied the group, an exception grudgingly allowed in order to secure both parent's skills as well as to satisfy the requirements for habitat-colony designation under AISMPE rules.

The colonists were subjected to extensive medical pre-screening before being allowed to apply for residency. The pre-screening was out of medical necessity, as the colonists would be out of range of the earth for extended periods of time, with only basic colonial medical bays and freezers of medication available to treat the sick.

Each colonist was under contract assignment with the Embraes company and would be required to work 9-hour shifts, six days a week, to prepare the colony for later expansion.

Unlike the orbital stations and Lunar colonies, which maintain an Earth-standard 24-hour clock cycle, a solar day on Mars lasts 24 hours, 39 minutes, and 35 seconds.

For the sake of familiarity, the colony planners opted to maintain as close as possible the Earth-standard 24-hour clock cycle on Mars. The additional 39 minutes, 35 seconds was designated as the "short hour" or "25th hour", and was scheduled to occur daily after midnight. The additional time partially off-set the colonist's lengthy work day.

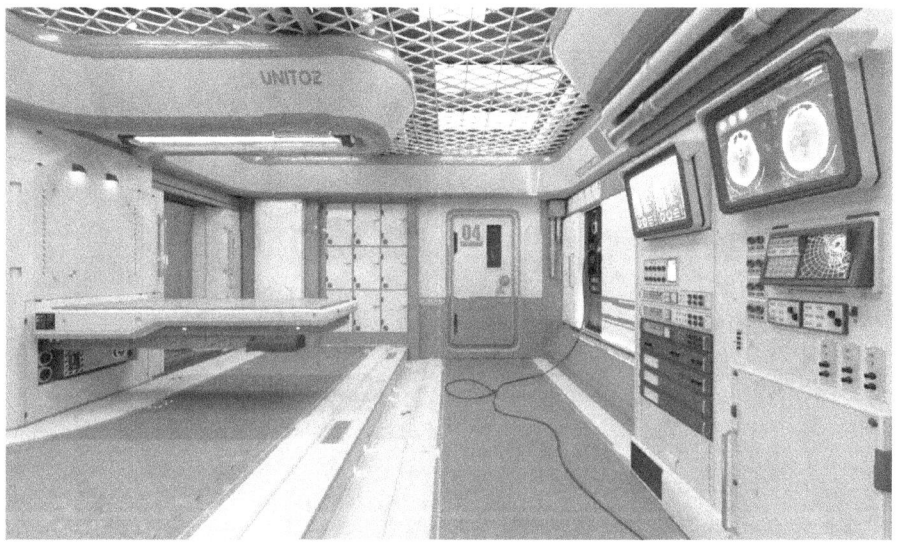

Figure 55 - Arch-Gale Colony Medical Bay Number 2, Level 4, circa 2108. Image courtesy AISMPE Colonial Archives, File 122013.

By design, the colonists were the last to transit through the FTN system. With all construction now completed and the last supplies stored, the 852 colonists transited to Mars on January 8, 2100.

By January 15, 2100, the Earth's orbit had moved the FTN network beyond the range of the colony's EPM platforms.

Delbert Arch

At 09:36 on March 12, 2101, bistatic radar equipment on

Eastern Hill reported the approach of a dust storm of significant size. Gale colony weather specialist Amanda Silva issued an alert to all surface teams to either return to the primary habitat or shelter in place at one of the colony's four remote emergency shelters.

Figure 56 - Senior Electrical Engineer, Delbert Arch, interacting with his personal SDU, "Jake", an older FANUC Series-2 SDU that accompanied Arch to Mars. Photo taken inside Recreation Center No. 1, Arch-Gale Colony, Mars, September 7, 2100. Image courtesy Estate of Lana Arch.

Three members of Engineering Group 4, led by Senior Electrical Engineer Delbert Arch, were at that moment repairing one of the colony's four "ice moles" in the Southern Tableland region of the crater. The team immediately set the mole to burrow under the surface and prepared to return in their rover.

Before the engineering group could reach the primary habitat, however, the storm breached the crater to the east and began spilling dust and sand into the basin. The closest shelter was Shelter 2, near Yellowknife Bay, approximately 6 kilometers from the habitat structure to the north. After reporting their arrival, the team sealed the shelter's doors and prepared to wait out the storm.

At approximately 11:20, the lights inside the primary habitat dimmed momentarily, then resumed their normal illumination. In the operation center, however, power technicians were alerted that all outlying manufacturing and auxiliary buildings were reporting a loss of power.

At 12:08, the water distillation plant shut down. At the same time, the power inside Shelter 2 went out. The engineers inside the shelter activated their remote suit lights and were checking the shelter's equipment when the shelter's auxiliary batteries engaged. From a quick review of the shelter's power systems, the engineers quickly deduced that the Shelter was no longer receiving power from the colony's fusion reactors, and had therefore engaged its emergency backup systems.

Operations Manager Jonathan Biggs signaled Governor Almeida's office and then sounded an alert. Within the habitat structure, all personnel immediately reported to their duty stations while technicians inside the operations center frantically searched for a reason for the power shut downs.

Inside Shelter 2, Delbert Arch was studying the power system layout for the shelter when he noted a reference to FR3, meaning the shelter received power from the fusion reactors based on the shelter being assigned a priority level of 3.

By design, the colony's four fusion reactors had been programmed to prioritize the delivery of power throughout the colony based on each receiving system's level of criticality.

Figure 57 - Senior Electrical Engineer, Delbert Arch, interacting with his personal SDU, "Jake", inside Recreation Center No. 1 on Mars. Image courtesy Estate of Lana Arch.

All external manufacturing buildings were lowest on the scale of criticality, rating a "4" priority level.

The external water treatment plant and the external emergency shelters rated a priority level of "3", being more important than the manufacturing facilities.

The CO_2 solid oxide electrolysis plants, designed to replenish the colony's oxygen, was the next most important system, rating priority level "2".

Finally, the habitat's heating plants, communications, operations center, and reserve O_2 systems were rated as priority level "1", or the most important systems.

Given the order at which the power outages had occurred, Arch speculated the fusion plants themselves might be shutting down and were prioritizing the remaining power according to the colony's critical system allocation schedule. Arch relayed this suspicion to the operations center.

In the operations center, technicians confirmed Arch's findings. Based on current power levels, they speculated that at least two of the colony's four fusion reactors had failed, despite having received no warnings from the reactor's controllers. Even more troubling, a third reactor was reporting wildly varying power spikes, indicating some type of controller failure was in progress.

Despite the raging storm, Arch instructed the other members of his team to remain behind and then exited the shelter. Alone in the maintenance rover, and guided solely by the crater's positioning beacons, Arch slowly proceeded toward the reactor farm.

Inside the operations center, technicians could only listen, helpless, as Arch described what he found.

When they had been installed, the four fusion reactors had been situated facing each other to permit technicians to service all four of the controllers from a single scaffold deck. A pressurized cryogenic tank left on an upper platform during a maintenance cycle had fallen to the deck in the storm and exploded. Fragments of the canister had punctured Reactor 2's controller housing and severed its cryogenic processor circuitry.

Without cryogenics to contain Reactor 2's plasma, the unit had begun to superheat. Escaping plasma had caused the coils to stop superconducting. The energy of the magnetic field, now converted into heat, had boiled off the remaining cryogens and had cooked the reactor's control processor. This "quench" had effectively shut down Reactor 2's magnetic and cryogenic systems. The superheated plasma had erupted, shooting across the scaffold deck directly towards Reactor 4's control box.

After several minutes, the superheated plasma had melted Reactor 4's protective box's casing and destroyed its internal controller. Reactor 4 now experienced its own "quench" and had begun discharging its own superheated plasma across the deck.

With both reactor control processors destroyed, no warning had been sent to the operations center. Meanwhile, the two damaged reactors, both venting superheated plasma at each other across the controller platform, threatened to destroy the remaining two reactor's controllers. Reactor 1's controller casing was already melting in proximity to the plasma fountains, and its controller, though still functioning, was shorting and sending overload warnings to the operation's center.

The situation was desperate. If all four reactor controllers failed, the colonists would slowly freeze, choking to death as CO_2 slowly built up inside the habitat dome.

Arch worked quickly to shut down Reactors 2 and 4. Once shut down, he then began repairing Reactor 1's damaged controller.

At 14:12, technicians within the operations center reported Reactor 1's power had stabilized.

Arch, however, failed to return to Shelter 2 or respond to subsequent radio communication. 16 hours later, with the storm now sufficiently abated, rescue and emergency maintenance teams were dispatched to the reactor farm.

Arch's body was found partially buried in the sand approximately 20 meters from Reactor 1's lower housing assembly.

After shutting down Reactors 2 and 4 and re-setting Reactor 1's controller, Arch's suit had been punctured by a damaged piece of scaffolding as he was descending from the platform in the blinding storm. He had become disoriented from lack of oxygen while attempting to locate the maintenance rover, fallen to the ground, and suffocated.

Delbert Arch was the first person to die on Mars.

In recognition of his sacrifice, the colony residents later voted to rename the colony the "Arch-Gale Colony". The proposal was passed unanimously at the first Mars Colonial Assembly meeting held on June 10, 2101.

The Delbert Arch Memorial can be visited today in the place where Arch's body was discovered, near to what was the site of the colony's original fusion reactor farm.

Arch's birthday is a local holiday for residents of the Arch-Gale colony (*See: "Delbert Arch: A Hero Among Us" – by Amanda Silva; NAFS-Archive Unit 119, 21p - (ar) 2104, File: AECF9EFF75*).

End Summary File: A3038951DB//:QKDS-51676F54A

Producer's Note: On February 21, 2018, our office facilitated a meeting between Mr. Clifton and two experts in the field of quantum theory and mathematics; Mitch Saito, a professor of theoretical physics, and Richard Alvis, a member of the International Association of Mathematical Physicists. The meeting took place at our company's office in New York.

Approximately four hours into the meeting, the parties were interrupted by agents from the United States Department of Energy. All electronic recording devices and notes evident in the meeting were seized by the Department of Energy representatives, who also detained and removed Mr. Clifton and his equipment from our office.

An audio recording from that meeting was later recovered from a cell phone concealed by one of our staff. From that recording, our invited experts were able to reconstruct much of the mathematical formulas and other information presented by Mr. Clifton at the meeting. The following are excerpts from that audio recording.

Technical Appendix

Clarification re: Negative Energy

[Alvis: One of the problems mathematicians have had with negative energy is that it is not definitively stated. Mathematicians like clear, precise equations, and so far, no one has been able to clearly define what negative energy actually is.]

I understand.

[Alvis: So, how would you define negative energy?]

The energy content of any region is given in terms of a stress-energy tensor equation. That is true whether we're talking about a physical region or a mathematical region.

[Alvis: True.]

Negative energy, however, cannot be defined within general relativity.

[Alvis: Why not?]

General relativity is too broad a concept to accommodate every possible scenario involving every form of energy. There are simply too many things that can impact the energy contained within a region. For example, it can differ depending on what type of matter or gravimetric fields are present.

[Alvis: Ok. I follow that.]

Physicists in your time attempted to draw conclusions about what must be allowed and disallowed in general relativity, by applying restrictions, which they called "energy conditions", on the tensor energy measurement for a region.

[Alvis: Ok.]

[Saito: Yes. That's true.]

Well, the problem with that is the fact that there is an infinite number of factors that can impact the energy in a region. So, when physicists tried to reconcile the stress-energy tensor measurements of one region with general relativity, they had to apply energy conditions to that region, but those same energy conditions might fail when they tried to apply them to another region.

[Alvis: I see.]

[Saito: Are you saying that no special energy conditions truly exist?]

I'm saying that the existence of a stabilized singularity does not violate general relativity if you begin with the correct stress-energy tensor equation.

The force that maintains and keeps a singularity within space-time can be reconciled with general relativity without applying any special energy conditions.

If you begin with the premise that all things that can impact the stress-energy tensor within a given region must be quantifiable, then negative energy is merely a force opposing positive energy.

[Alvis: That's precisely what I'm saying... the definition is too general.]

Yes, but you asked me to describe negative energy, not a specific form of negative energy.

[Alvis: What do you mean?]

Well, how would you describe energy?

[Alvis: Ah! I see what you mean. There are many different kinds of energy, such as thermal energy, radiant energy, kinetic energy, electrical energy...]

Precisely. The term "energy" is too broad. It describes a multitude of different types of energy.

In the same way, the term "negative energy" is also too broad. There are many forms of negative energy.

[Alvis: I see.]

[Saito: Ok then, let's get specific. What form of negative energy do you use to keep the wormhole open?]

Actually, we don't use negative energy to maintain our singularity.

[Saito: Impossible. You must have some form of negative energy

pushing from the inside or the wormhole would collapse.]

Do you recall me mentioning our singularity has both a near and a distant horizon?

[Saito: Yes.]

And do you recall me saying that these two event horizons are quantum entangled?

[Saito: Yes.]

When we form our singularity, manipulations of the electromagnetic field cause a quantum separation to occur at the moment of generation.

[Saito: What do you mean, a separation?]

The singularity is separated, at the quantum level, into two distinct event horizons, which we call the near and distant horizons. Both of these horizons are still quantum entangled, connected to each other at the quantum level.

[Saito: Oh my God!]

Do you understand what I'm saying?

[Saito: You're connecting TWO wormholes... two wormholes that are part of the same wormhole!]

Precisely.

[Saito: Oh my God!]

[Alvis: I don't understand. Why is that significant?]

[Saito: It solves the problem of negative energy!]

That is correct. We don't need to have a negative energy force keeping the event horizons open. The force we use to keep our singularity stable is actually generated from outside the singularity, by the tensor assembly's electromagnetic field.

We learned from the Luyteni that adding certain interactions couples the boundaries of quantum-entangled Schwarzschild anti-de Sitter singularities. This results in a quantum matter stress tensor with a negative average null energy, rendering it traversable after gravitational backreaction.

[Saito: So, the tunnel is simply the quantum entangled state that exists between the two event horizons! You don't have to create the tunnel! It's already there!]

Yes. The stress tensor assembly separates the singularity at the quantum level, and these form the tunnel between the now-separated event horizons.

The electromagnetic force separating the event horizons also has a repulsing effect, keeping the two event horizons open.

It also prevents Hawking radiation from being excreted from the singularity, which if allowed to escape, would exhaust and collapse the singularity.

[Alvis: It sounds similar to a process math theorists call quantum

teleportation, which is proposed under the theory of quantum cryptography... and that actually has already been proved under laboratory conditions.]

Yes. It is similar.

Early physicists theorized about joining wormholes to facilitate transition, but they couldn't determine how to actually join them together.

What we learned from the Luyteni is how to separate and couple a single singularity at the quantum level, rather than attempting to join two different singularities together. This solved the problem of quantum coupling as well as allowing for both spatial and quantum manipulation of the event horizons through the principle of entanglement.

[Saito: And particle entanglement allows you to manipulate both sides of the wormhole.]

Yes. Quantum engineers in my time call this "reflection" because the manipulations to the electromagnetic field constraining the quantum-entangled ions within the EPM containment unit are reflected in the singularity's event horizons, even though one of those horizons, the distant horizon, might be thousands of kilometers away or 100 years in the past. Einstein called the phenomenon "spooky action at a distance".

[Saito: So, there really is no negative energy keeping your singularity open?]

Not in the way you think of negative energy. Once the

micro-singularity has been formed, the tensor's latitudinal arms manipulate the electromagnetic field against the singularity. It prevents the singularity from being pushed out of space-time. It separates and couples the singularity at the quantum level and then repositions the two coupled event horizons outside of the containment unit.

[Saito: How do you resolve the averaged null energy violation of an object moving through your wormhole?]

Violation of the averaged null energy condition is actually a prerequisite for all traversable wormholes, but that does not make such transit impossible.

There must be infinite null geodesics passing through the wormhole, with tangent vector k^μ and affine parameter λ, along which:

$$\int_{-\infty}^{+\infty} T_{\mu\nu}\kappa^\mu\kappa^\nu d\lambda < 0$$

Objects can pass through the directly coupled boundaries. The causal structure of the singularity's manifold is modified as a result, changing the commutation relations along null geodesics through the tunnel and making them no longer achronal.

For the same reason, a causal horizon extending through the wormhole intersects itself, removing the piece with the divergent area. Hence the above impossibility results do not apply. In effect, what you thought was impossible, is possible under the right tensor model.

T. E. WILLIS

[Saito: So, no negative energy is used, but you achieve the same result as if you had employed negative energy.]

That's a fair statement. The energy in our configuration is similar to the Casimir effect, which, as you know, is a negative energy principle. It is similar in that the interaction between the boundaries implies that the radial direction is effectively a compact circle.

It is helpful to remember that a small spherically symmetric perturbation of the stress tensor $T_{\mu\nu} \sim O(\epsilon)$ will result in a traversable singularity exactly when the averaged null energy condition is violated, by solving the linearized Einstein equation for $h_{\mu\nu} = \delta g_{\mu\nu} \sim O(\epsilon)$.

[Alvis: In one of the summary files I read, someone named Dean comes up with a formula to calculate the energy density required to move an object through the wormhole.]

Yes. Nigel Dean. We call that formula "Dean's Formula".

[Alvis: Right. I saw the formula next to a picture in one of the summary files you sent, but can you describe the math behind the integrated null energy he used to derive his formula?]

Certainly. The integrated null energy formula is:

$$\int_{U_0}^{\infty} dU\, T_{UU} = -4h\Delta C_0 \int_{U_0}^{\infty} dU_{U \to U}^{\lim} \partial_U G\left(U, U'; U_o\right)$$

where $G\left(U, U'; U_0\right)$ is identical to:

$$\int_{U_0}^{U} dU_1 \int_{1}^{\frac{U}{U_1}} \frac{dy}{\sqrt{y^2 - 1}} \frac{U_1^{\Delta}}{(U - U_1 y)^{\Delta} (U U_1' + y)^{\Delta+1}}$$

[Alvis: Got it. Thank you... and if we turn off the interaction at U_f, then what is the integral?]

It is just the difference between $\displaystyle\int_{U_0}^{\infty} dU\, T_{UU}$ and $\displaystyle\int_{U_f}^{\infty} dU\, T_{UU}$.

[Alvis: Perfect. Thank you.]

225

Exotic Phased Matter

[Saito: I'd like to talk more about the exotic phased matter you use.]

Very well.

[Saito: In the files you sent, you mentioned "electron-depleted osmium" and "osmium ions". Can you tell me why osmium is used?]

From the Luyteni signals, quantum engineers understood that they needed to be able to contain a micro-singularity within a material with very specific properties.

The material needed to be very dense, at least as dense as molybdenum.

To be used in a device operated by human beings, it also needed to be radioactively stable.

It needed to be capable of superconducting.

Finally, it needed to be relatively strong, to support internal pressure from a vacuum without implosion.

From these constraints, early quantum engineers considered using rhenium, ruthenium, and osmium.

Rhenium was ruled out as being far too expensive. In addition, the question of its toxicity was also a factor in its disqualification.

Ruthenium was seriously considered. It was more common than rhenium, was stable, super-conducting, and contained sufficient electrons to permit sufficient compression under electromagnetic fields.

Ultimately, however, osmium was selected over ruthenium simply because of osmium's numerically-superior number of shell electrons. While both elements contained the same number of electrons in their first 3 electron shells (2, 8, and 18), osmium's fourth electron shell contained more than twice the number as ruthenium's (32 for osmium, 15 for ruthenium).

[Saito: Why would the number of electrons be an important factor?]

The answer to that is two-fold.

First, the EPM containment unit must be constructed of an electron-depleted material in order to create a strong positive ionic charge inside the unit. This also increases the material's density. So, there must be enough electrons available to remove from the element to create a sufficiently positive ionic charge.

Second, the singularity itself is formed using ions from the same element, compressed by an electromagnetic field, until the remaining electrons are cast off inside the unit. This "casting off" of the element's remaining electrons is precisely measured by the tensor assembly and is a key variable used to calibrate the electromagnetic field's gravimetric compression.

So, the element selected must have sufficient electrons to support both depletion of those electrons from its containment unit in order to give the unit a strong positive ionic charge, while at the same time allowing for electron "cast off" to occur under compression to aid in calibration.

Osmium has enough electrons to fulfill both requirements.

[Saito: Why must the container have a strong positive ionic charge?]

It assists the tensor assembly with calibrating the singularity. The tensor assembly must precisely manipulate an electromagnetic field against a collection of ions spinning at nearly the speed of light, inside a chamber composed of the same elemental material. A strong positive ionic charge helps the tensor assembly distinguish between the ions being compressed, and the ions within the containment material.

The EPM containment unit's ionic charge fluctuates between positive and negative based on a singularity inside either casting off or retaining electrons under electromagnetic compression.

As the containment unit captures "cast off" electrons, its positive ionic state is reduced. Eventually, the containment unit will capture more electrons than normally exists within its native substrate material, and the ionic state of the containment unit then reports as negative.

How to Build a Time Machine

[Saito: So, if someone wanted to recreate your MTY process today, could they do it?]

I believe so, but with certain obvious caveats.

Sufficient power to form the singularity can be generated using nuclear power technology. In fact, the first singularity at the P-SEQS facility near Geneva was generated using only nuclear power.

A control processor capable of instantaneously performing numerous extremely complex calculations would also be required. In June of this year, your government's Department of Energy and the IBM company will announce the world's fastest supercomputer, called the Summit. That unit will be capable of performing 200,000 trillion calculations per second, which should be sufficient to manage the quantum and spatial formula calculations. It would be slow, but it would be possible.

[Saito: What about the containment unit. Your unit is fractured.]

Yes, the containment unit would be a challenge. Essentially, you need to be able to accelerate osmium ions at a speed much faster than you can at present. Then, you'd need to contain them within an electron-depleted osmium sphere using an electromagnetic field properly interacting with a time-varying current, to produce the gravimetric energy needed to sustain the space-time singularity's co-generation process.

[Saito: So, we can't do it?]

Perhaps you can. The first singularity was generated using an early third generation KEK-GenQ quantum-TeV ion accelerator. That device was based on a linear accelerator approach first conceived by the SLAC National Accelerator Laboratory at Stanford University in 2017. The SLAC researchers will shortly announce they have discovered a method of reducing both the size and increasing the speed, of a particle accelerator. That breakthrough will ultimately allow particle accelerators to be reduced to meters, rather than kilometers, while also greatly increasing the speed of acceleration.

[Saito: How will they do that?]

Instead of shooting electrons down a copper vacuum tube and pushing them along with microwaves, they will propel the electrons through a precisely-engineered silica chip, and then excite them with laser emissions.

The electrons will first be accelerated to nearly the speed of light using a conventional linear accelerator. Then, they will then be shot through a half-micron tall channel etched into a silica chip.

The channel will have a series of ridges and troughs carved into it. By varying the width of these ridges with respect to the wavelength of the laser, they will be able to generate a net energy gain as the electrons pass through the chip. The chip's acceleration gradient, which measures the amount of energy added to the electron as it travels a specific distance, will be at least 700 megavolts per meter (MeV/m). That would be sufficient to generate a singularity, though the calibration will take considerable time given the accelerator limitations. With sufficient nuclear power to sustain the process, you should be able to form a singularity of… oh… perhaps 1 meter.

[Saito: You say they built such an accelerator last year?]

No. They announced their theoretical design model last year, and they are working on the prototype now.

[Saito: Ok, so how could we recreate the containment unit?]

Creating an electron-depleted osmium sphere is not impossible. It's just difficult. The real challenge will be to create one that is perfectly spherical and then maintain a near QED vacuum within it.

You could create a near-perfect sphere using a small manufacturing plant operated in a zero-gravity environment. So…

[Saito: You mean, we'd have to construct it at the international space station?]

Well, yes, that's one method that might work. The closest man has come to creating a perfect sphere on the earth in your time was in 2008. The Australian Center for Precision Optics crafted a sphere of silicon with less than 0.3 nanometers of deviation, from special silicon crystals.

The silicon was purified in centrifuges once used to refine uranium for nuclear weapons. The centrifuges separated the silicon by isotope, allowing researchers to create a remarkably pure batch of silicon-28.

You could use a similar process to try and craft an osmium sphere, but the challenge would be to shape both the internal chamber as a perfect sphere, as well as the external shell, and do it without deviation or variation in the thickness of the shell.

Not an easy task.

[Saito: No! Not an easy task to be sure!]

But if you can do that, then the rest is simple. I can transmit the quantum and spatial equations for your control unit from my MTY's quantum controller, and show you how to construct the tensor assembly using conventional electromagnetic field generators. The same holds true for the tunneling regulator. The engineering can be accomplished using equipment available in this time.

With the right tensor equations, a fast control processor, and enough power behind it, you should be able to generate and contain a singularity.

[Saito: But that won't help you, will it?]

No. It won't help me get back, because, as I explained earlier, the gravimetric force that forms the singularity pushes its event horizons out of normal space-time, backward, not forward. So, even if we built a working version of an MTY device, we'd only be able to go backward and then return to the point from which we left. There's no way to build one here and have it take someone forward in time.

Singularity Generation

[Saito: Can you tell me what actually occurs at the moment a wormhole is created inside the osmium sphere?]

A singularity is formed when protons, spinning at nearly the speed of light inside the containment unit, have been compressed to the point where they begin to collide, forming a gravitational field on the surface of the compressed ion's nucleus, warping space-time within the unit.

[Saito: Yes, I follow that. What I'm trying to understand is what actually happens inside the sphere, step by step? What happens from the moment the device is hooked up?]

First, the EPM containment unit requires a near-QED vacuum environment. Of course, achieving a true absolute vacuum is not physically possible.

[Saito: Of course]

We achieve a near QED vacuum, however, by electromagnetically expelling all matter from the containment unit and the collider coils before charging begins.

Of course, to achieve that near-QED vacuum state and maintain near-c ion rotation inside the unit, the electromagnetic field must not be impinged in any way, which means the containment unit must be capable of superconducting.

The EPM containment unit is maintained at superconducting temperatures using an HTS cuprate-perovskite ceramic heat sink placed at the base of the EPM's unit housing where it is seated inside the MTY device. The heat sink is powered by the fusion reactor. Once the EPM unit's internal temperature reaches between -203.15 and -183.15 Celsius, then proton acceleration may begin.

[Saito: Ok.]

The ions are accelerated on the collider floor... Did I mention the singularity can only be generated on the collider floor? An MTY device cannot generate enough power to form a singularity.

[Saito: Yes, you mentioned that.]

Very well. So, the ions are accelerated to nearly the speed of light and then injected into the EPM containment unit. The EPM unit is already superconducting and electromagnetically charged, so the tensor assembly takes over at that point to maintain the particle rotation.

[Saito: I see.]

The tensor assembly's latitudinal arms, under power from the reactors on the collider floor, now begin their electromagnetic compression. Within a few seconds, to a few minutes, depending on the quantum and/or spatial coordinates supplied to the controller, the spinning osmium ions cast off their remaining electrons and begin to collide. When that occurs, the P(E) display begins dropping.

At the moment the singularity forms, all remaining electrons are expelled from the compressed ions, and the P(E) abruptly drops to negative. At that point, the singularity has been formed, but not yet calibrated to the proper space or time.

Without the tensor assembly's countervailing force, the singularity would vanish, tunneling backward through space-time as it exhausted itself from within through Hawking radiation excretion.

[Saito: Ok.]

The tensor assembly arrests that process, and now begins oscillating the electromagnetic field, causing the singularity to be squeezed, or separated, into distinct event horizons, connected at the quantum level.

[Saito: Oscillating?]

Well, that isn't an accurate description, I admit. The actual waveform manipulation is extremely complex and variable-rich. For lack of an easier description, we refer to it as oscillation. The important thing to understand is that, at this point, what was one singularity is now two quantum-entangled event horizons of the same singularity.

[Saito: Ok. Please continue.]

At this point, based on the spatial or temporal coordinates, the tensor assembly calibrates the negative average null energy needed to permit an object to transit the singularity's two event horizons. For distant transits, and for temporal transits, more energy is required to achieve calibration.

When temporal coordinates are supplied, the tunneling

regulator assists the tensor with determining the precise quantum settings, taking into account such variables as the planet's orbit over time. Of course, for simple EPM transitions, no tunneling regulator is necessary.

When calibration has been completed, the singularity is ready but remains in its micro-state until dilation.

At that point, the MTY device's internal fusion reactor maintains the singularity in its micro-state until it is dilated at the on-site tripback or EPM platform location.

[Saito: Thank you. That was much clearer.]

Gravimetric Plate Manufacturing

[Saito: You mentioned gravimetric plates being used on orbital stations. I would like to discuss that for a moment.]

Certainly.

[Saito: Can you explain how that works please?]

Very well. As I'm sure you know, all atoms are composed of electrons, protons, and neutrons. Electrons have such a small mass that we can disregard them as contributing to gravity.

Protons and neutrons are composed of three quarks, tightly bound together by gluons. The gluons are the carriers of a strong nuclear force that binds the quarks together.

If you add up the mass of the three quarks that make up a proton or neutron, however, you would only end up with approximately 1 percent of the total particle's mass.

The remaining 99 percent of the particle's mass is comprised of the gluon's binding energy that holds the quarks together. It is the gluon's binding energy that makes up most of what we call gravity.

[Saito: Yes. I am familiar with that principle.]

What the Luyteni shared with man was the concept of perturbation of that gluon's binding energy using electromagnetic fields. Essentially, the gluon's strong nuclear force can be affected, without increasing the number of quarks... that is... without increasing the number of protons or neutrons.

*[Saito: To affect a gluon's binding energy, you must have more mass...
that is... more protons or neutrons.]*

With enough particle mass, you would have enough gluon binding energy, that is true.

If you could construct a platform between the Earth and Luna composed of pure neutron particles, for example, such a dense-mass object would have the gravitational pull of the Earth.

Unfortunately, with such enormous mass, it would also gravitationally attract the moon, just like the Earth does now, and the close proximity of such an object between the Earth and the moon would likely pull the two bodies together.

So, while increasing mass *can* generate near-Earth gravity, it's not a practical solution for an orbiting space station.

[Saito: I agree.]

The Luyteni helped us to understand how to increase the strength of the gluon's binding energy within a confined electromagnetic field, without increasing its underlying particle mass.

[Saito: How?]

Let's start with the basic field generator plate design.

A generator plate is created by stacking multiple layers of superconducting sheets containing millions of nano-anti-Helmholtz coils. Each sheet increases the gluon's binding energy for the sheets above, exponentially increasing until 1g has been achieved at the top sheet.

What we accomplish is similar to the Casimir effect. If you take two electrically conducting sheets and put them very close together, the sheets affect the empty space in between them in such a way as to create a negative energy density. By stacking a precise number of such sheets and applying an electrical charge, we generate a field at the top sheet with the same order of magnitude as a gravitational wave signal.

The millions of coils on each sheet are constructed of two solenoids with a radius l_i ($l_i < l$), with length L, and separated by distance D. An electric current is then applied to the opposing coils.

[Alvis: Can you give us the actual gravitational field equations?]

Certainly. First, let's start with the field limit gravitational equations. Understanding that $a_{rel} \ll a_{pf}$ and $\rho, \lambda \ll 1$, then the formulas I described earlier can be simplified as:

$$\nabla^2 \rho = \frac{C_I}{U^2} \frac{L^2}{l^2} \left(\left(\partial_u a_{pf} \right)^2 + \frac{l^2}{L^2} \left(\partial_v a_{pf} \right)^2 \right)$$

and

$$\nabla^2 \lambda = \frac{C_I}{U^2} \frac{L^2}{l^2} \left(\left(\partial_u a_{pf} \right)^2 + \frac{l^2}{L^2} \left(\partial_v a_{pf} \right)^2 \right)$$

where

$$\nabla^2 = \partial \frac{2}{u} + \frac{1}{u} \partial_u + \frac{l^2}{L^2} \partial \frac{2}{v}$$

As I mentioned earlier, the source of each plate's electromagnetic field is the stacked nano-anti-Helmholtz coils.

The coils are laid down at a quantum-manufacturing plant in a grid pattern, on a superconducting nano-etchable sheet.

Each plate must contain sufficient coiled sheets to produce a space-time curvature when an electrical current on the order of 10^4 A per cm^2 is applied to the individual sheets.

At 8 coils per square micrometer (μm), 74 stacked sheets will generate a curvature equivalent to 1g per square nanometer on the plate, to a height of 5 meters. When nano-spaced at 8 coils per square micrometer (μm), 166 stacked sheets will radiate a gravimetric wave equivalent to 1g to a height of 8 meters.

The equation for calculating the total magnetic potential a_{pf} of number of coils p with radius l_i is:

$$a_{pf} = \sum_{i=1}^{p} \left(a_{pf}^{slo} \left(f, z + \frac{D}{2}; l_i \right) - a_{pf}^{slo} \left(f, z - \frac{D}{2}; l_i \right) \right)$$

[Alvis: Got it. Thank you.]

[Saito: Can the same method be applied to negate gravity... to create an anti-gravity force?]

Yes. Pairs of precisely imbalanced nano-anti-Helmholtz coils produce a vertical magnetic field gradient that disrupts or counteracts a gravimetric wave signal.

[Saito: You mentioned a 'superconducting nano-etchable sheet'. What material is used to create the sheet?]

The first gravimetric coil sheets were constructed using a niobium-titanium (Nb-Ti) alloy, however, they were simply too cost prohibitive for mass-production and they were difficult to micro-print. Magnesium diboride (MgB2) was also tried, but when manufactured thin enough to permit nano-etching, it proved unable to carry the electrical load required by the solenoids.

Eventually, designers settled on sheets of single-walled carbon nanotube. They discovered that, with the smaller tube diameters, the greater curvature of the tube increased the interaction between the electrons and lattice vibrations, or phonons, which as you know is an essential property for superconductivity.

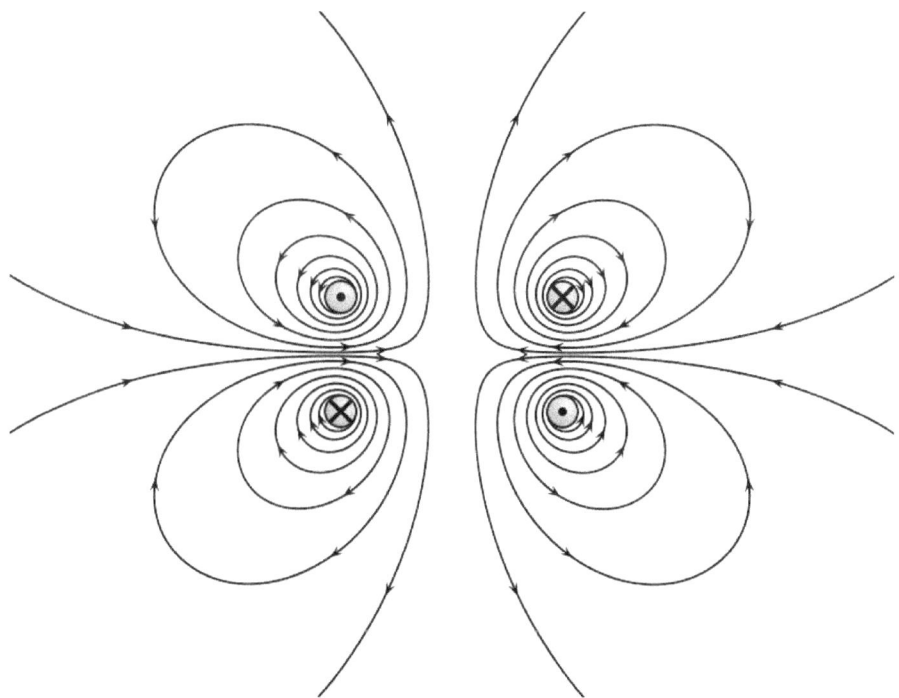

Figure 58 - Magnetic flow within an anti-Helmholtz coil.

The sheet's length-to-diameter ratio was 132,000,000-to-1, meaning it had a tensile strength greater than steel, conductivity far greater than copper, and thermal dissipation greater than diamonds. It also resisted corrosion and fatigue.

The unique nature of the carbon's molecular structure also allowed the nano-anti-Helmholtz coils to be printed directly onto the carbon sheets using a two-photon polymerization micro-printing process.

[Saito: How long does it take the stacked sheets to accumulate enough phase shift to reach the same magnitude as a gravitational wave signal?]

Well, that's all about the amount of power put into the coils, isn't it?

[Saito: True... but given the superconducting nature of your carbon sheet, I assume you there is a formula to calculate the phase shift based on current?]

True. The phase shift along the axis of each coil for one cycle is derived as:

$$\Delta\Phi = \frac{\pi}{\Lambda} \int_0^{\mathscr{L}} (\rho(0,z) - \lambda(0,z))dz$$

The nano-anti-Helmholtz coils generate a maximum curvature of space-time at mid-distance from each of the solenoids, where $(u = 0, v = 0)$. That's the point where the magnetic field vanishes.

The field is maximized at the center of the solenoids, at

$$\left(z = \pm \frac{D}{2} \right)$$

When an electrical current of 10^4 A per cm² is applied to a sheet containing 8 coils per square micrometer (μm), the accumulated phase shift at the top of the 74 sheets reaches $\Delta\varnothing \approx -1.08 \times 10^{-11}$ within approximately 0.42 seconds.

That value has the same order of magnitude as a gravitational wave signal.

[Saito: Amazing!]

[Alvis: Can you give me the formula to create an imbalance in the gravimetric field? To create an anti-gravity force?]

Certainly, let's begin with the field limit gravitational equations again…

Producer's Note: At this moment, the meeting was interrupted by agents from the U.S. Department of Energy, who removed Mr. Clifton, his device, and all notes, cameras, and recording devices evident in the room.

Final Emails

Producer's Note: Approximately 3 hours after Mr. Clifton was removed from our office, our executive producer received the first of three brief emails from Clifton. These emails are printed in their entirety below.

Email at Leesburg Executive Airport

From: ******** <********@********>
Date: February 21, 2018 at 02:11:45 PM EST
To: ******** <******** @********>
Subject:

This is John Clifton.

I am sending this through my datstem.

The men who removed me from your office informed me we would be transporting by helicopter. I had never flown in one before, and I naturally assumed the experience would be similar to an old 4-rotor transport drone.

I flew in one of those once when I was a young man.

The experience was nothing like I expected. It was so loud I couldn't hear anyone speaking, and the vibration was simply terrifying.

We've landed at a small aerial transport station. I'll try and find out where I am.

They have removed the restraints around my wrists.

I am in Leesburg, Virginia. I see that name on one of the aerial station building signs. I don't think this is a commercial transit station. It appears too small. It has only 50 or 60 small aerial transports here.

They had ground transports waiting. I have asked several times where we are going, but they have refused to answer my questions.

We are in a large grey ground transport. They secured my MTY device in a container inside the back of the transport. In addition to myself, the man with the dark hair who detained me at your office is also here. The other men who came to your office left in a different transport.

There were two other men waiting at the aerial station when we landed and they are in the transport with us. One of them is driving the unit. The other and the man with the dark hair who detained me at your office are sitting on either side of me inside the transport.

We just passed a sign that said "Leesburg Executive Airport", so that must be where we landed.

The transport operator is speaking with someone on a handheld communication device.

We just entered onto a transway called "Dulles Greenway". We're moving generally south-east.

The man on the communication device just told someone that we would "be there in 40 minutes".

Once I discover where they are taking me, I will send another communication.

Email from inside Forrestal Building

From: ******** <********@********>
Date: February 21, 2018 at 09:01:15 PM EST
To: ******** <******** @********>
Subject:

This is John Clifton.

I am inside a building in Washington D.C. We exited the transport inside an underground parking facility, so I am not certain which building I am in. When we were taking the lift up inside the building, however, I noticed the name "Forrestal" on a maintenance plate below the control panel. My datstem suggests I am inside the "James Forrestal Building".

I have been in a room with between 20 and 30 individuals who have been questioning me for more than 5 hours.

I asked for something to eat about an hour ago, and they just brought me a tray of food. I am sending you this message while I am eating.

Most of the people questioning me are clearly not military personnel, but there are three men in the room wearing uniforms. I suspect that an older man in the room is also affiliated with the military, although he is not wearing a uniform. The uniformed personnel appear deferential towards him.

The people questioning me appear to be engineers or scientific technicians. They obviously come from a physics or mathematics background. Several appear to be knowledgeable in rudimentary quantum theory.

Three of the men who came to your office are also in the room, though the man with the dark hair who detained and transported me is not present.

When they first brought me into the room, an older man read a legal statement to me. Essentially, the statement said that, since I am not a citizen of the present United States, I cannot claim the exercise of those rights granted to its current citizens. He asked me if I understood that statement and then advised me to cooperate and sign the statement.

I assured him that, as long as I was not mistreated, I would be happy to cooperate. I signed the statement and he left the room.

My MTY device is not in the room with me. About an hour after we arrived, a man brought a number of printed images of the device and handed them to one of the men in the room. They have been showing me the images and asking me questions about the device's various components. They seem particularly interested in its fusion reactor, and also with its quantum control processor. In one of the images, I can see that the device controller's translucent shield has been removed, so it appears they are attempting to disassemble the device.

About an hour ago, one of the men in the room was querying me about the device's fusion reactor's data coupling to its quantum analytic processor. He asked if disconnecting the reactor's data coupler would damage the controller's quantum circuits.

I said, no, it wouldn't harm the controller but it would likely trigger a fusion detonation since the controller also maintains the reactor's cryogenics. When I said that, several of the men in the room left rather abruptly.

I have finished eating now so I will transmit this message while I am still able to do so. My datstem is reporting all incoming and outgoing communication routers into this building are being monitored, so I am transmitting this communication through a router my datstem has isolated within one of the nearby buildings.

Final Email

From: ******** <********@********>
Date: February 21, 2018 at 11:36:26 PM EST
To: ******** <******** @********>
Subject:

This is John Clifton again.

There are only a dozen men left in the room with me now.

I am very tired. I have asked the people here when I would be able to rest, and they have assured me that we will be leaving shortly.

I believe they are making preparations to transport me to a facility in Tennessee. I overheard one of the men on his hand communication device asking if everything was ready "at Oak Ridge". My datstem suggests that he was likely referring to Oak Ridge, Tennessee.

We appear to be taking a break now, so I will use this opportunity to transmit this message.

Producer's Note: Our office has received no further communications from Mr. Clifton. The following day, on February 22, 2018, our executive producer's access to his personal email account was blocked.

Department of Energy Press Release

Producer's note: The following press release was published by the Department of Energy on May 2, 2018, two months and twelve days after Mr. Clifton and his device were removed from our office.

See: https://www.energy.gov/articles/department-energy-invest-30-million-quantum-science-initiative

May 2, 2018

WASHINGTON, D.C. – Today, U.S. Secretary of Energy Rick Perry announced that the Department of Energy (DOE) plans to invest up to \$30 million over the next three years in Quantum Information Science (QIS).

QIS is a new, wide-ranging area of research that is expected to lay the groundwork for the next generation of computing and information processing, as well as an array of other innovative technologies.

This new initiative will provide up to \$10 million per year for three years on a competitive basis for research and new equipment at DOE's five Nanoscale Science Research Centers (NSRCs) located at DOE National Laboratories around the nation. It will enable these facilities to take their first steps into the new quantum era. Out-year funding will be dependent on congressional appropriations.

"Quantum Information Science represents the future in a wide range of fields from computing to physics to materials science, and it will play a major role in shaping the technologies of tomorrow," said Secretary Perry. "It's vital that American science and American scientists lead the way into this new era, and these planned investments in our DOE Nanoscale Science Research Centers are an important first step."

The NSRC QIS initiative is one of a series of funding awards in QIS that DOE's Office of Science plans for Fiscal Year 2018. Awards under these other solicitations are expected to provide additional funds in support of QIS research to institutions across the nation before the end of FY 2018.

The growing interest in QIS has been driven by both need and opportunity. The need comes from the slowing of Moore's Law—the famous 1965 prediction by Intel co-founder Gordon Moore that computing power would double each year (later amended to eighteen months) because of the doubling of transistors on microchips. In recent years, as the number of transistors per chip has approached physical limits, the doubling has slowed. The expectation is that at some point, such doubling will cease to be possible within the world of "classical physics," or the normal physical world.

This has led researchers to probe the world of "quantum physics," or subatomic reality, in search of alternative answers.

In the quantum world, it is possible for things to seem to be and not be at the same time, and to encounter what is called nonlocal effects.

The thought is that these strange quantum effects, phenomena such as "superposition" and "entanglement", may provide an alternative approach to information processing and other technologies.

This alternative opportunity has come from scientists' increasing ability to probe the quantum world with precision. The emergence of nano science and cutting-edge nano technology research facilities such as the NSRCs have provided a major starting point into quantum reality, which is why DOE is taking the next step in quantum studies.

The effort is expected to generate a multitude of new, exotic materials with unprecedented properties as well as contribute to the development of many new technologies.

NSRC users, which together serve a community of over 3,000 researchers from universities, National Laboratories, nonprofits, and industry annually are expected to benefit from the development of new NSRC capabilities that result from the QIS initiative.

The five NSRCs invited to submit proposals for QIS funding include:

- The Center for Nanoscale Materials at Argonne National Laboratory;
- The Center for Functional Nano materials at Brookhaven National Laboratory;
- The Molecular Foundry at Lawrence Berkeley National Laboratory;
- The Center for Nano phase Materials Sciences at Oak Ridge National Laboratory; and
- The Center for Integrated Nano technologies jointly managed by Sandia National Laboratory and Los Alamos Laboratory.

www.ingramcontent.com/pod-product-compliance
Lightning Source LLC
Chambersburg PA
CBHW071136260626
47162CB00003B/810